I0645917

Love Map

Love Map

A TRUE STORY OF SEXUAL DESIRE,
FANTASY, AND EXPLORATION
BETWEEN A YOUNGER MAN
AND AN OLDER WOMAN

• • •

Alice Ellison

Euphoric Publications, LLC

ISBN: 978-0-9989629-0-0 (E-Book)
ISBN: 9780998962917 (Print)
ISBN 10: 0998962910

Dedication

• • •

This book is dedicated to the man who inspired it. He knows who he is.

Table of Contents

"Reason is intelligence taking exercise.
Imagination is intelligence with an erection."

Victor Hugo

Preface

...

WHEN 34-YEAR OLD DECLAN MESSAGES Sara on an Internet dating platform, she thinks he doesn't realize her age. She's in her 50's. Unbeknownst to her, she is exactly what he's been searching for. Follow the pair as their minds become tightly tangled up together while developing a steamy relationship full of varied, erotic fantasy lived out in real time. Themes include: Younger Man/Older Woman, Sex with a Stranger, Bi-Sexuality, Varied Role Play, Power & Surrender, Domination & Submission, Exhibitionism, Voyeurism, and Incest Fantasy.

Introduction

• • •

As you read their text messages you become a voyeur of the sexual activity that develops between the lovers. The numbered days for the text conversations enable you to follow and understand how innocent and mundane talk quickly spirals into erotic adventure in theater of the mind. The relationship that evolves explores the human condition for a younger man and an older woman who randomly find each other and act out their erotic desires. Beyond adult literary escapism, this story may help you understand yourself, your partner, and the world around you. This is an engaging tale that will make you laugh, gasp, consider your own sexual desires, and want to get "busy" as quickly as possible.

What significance does the title of this book have to the story? A "Love Map" is a person's internal blueprint for an idealized lover and what, as a pair, you do together in the idealized, romantic, erotic, and sexualized relationship. You aren't born with a love map. It develops in early childhood and is unique to the individual, like an accent in a spoken language. Input from the senses and certain experiences in childhood shape the love map or mental template. So, for example, severe spankings from Dad and Mom walking around the house in her sexy underwear really can impact the young developing psyche. Once the love map forms, it's hard to alter. Interestingly, a person might not discover certain aspects of their love map until a significant experience triggers it later in life. The title is also a nod to the late John Money, the leading 20ᵗʰ Century sexologist who pioneered the theory and coined the term "lovemap" to explain how people develop their sexual preferences. He posits (and I'm severely paraphrasing here) that when something bad happens to you in childhood, such as deprivation and neglect, abusive punishment and discipline, or an experience that causes you to become genitally stimulated, it can really fuck you up, causing your love map to become "vandalized." As an adult, you may act out sexually in bizarre and kinky ways. It's possible to find a partner whose vandalized love map mirrors or reciprocates your own. With such a partner, fantasy that exists only in the imagination can be brought to life through action.

What's the difference between this story and something like *50 Shades of Grey* or *The Story of X*? You won't find a billionaire inviting you into his Italian mansion or an entrepreneur taking you for a ride in his private helicopter on these pages. No girl falling in love with a wealthy stranger who has a dark mysterious side. No wealthy and worldly man meeting a shy young girl with nothing to offer but her naivety. No seduction then indoctrination into the world of BDSM where she discovers her true nature is to be limitlessly submissive to whatever abuse pleases the sadist most. This is no romance novel. What you will find here is a book written like a private sexual journal displaying a great variety of fantasies and sexual interests. The woman in these pages is strong, smart, aggressive, and sexually creative. And this story could actually happen. In fact, it did.

CHAPTER 1

The Online Dating Thing

• • •

SOMETIMES THE UNIVERSE THROWS YOU something absolutely unexpected. It's like a cosmic curveball. And it hits you out of the blue. Whether it's a good thing or a bad one can't always be judged at the time it happens. This story is real. The events described here actually happened. Everything took place in Washington, D.C. during winter and spring of 2017. The names of the man and woman involved and some of the biographical information have been changed to protect their privacy. And that's the way it is, at least for now.

Sara is in her early 50's. She's had several long-term relationships. She's a serial monogamist. Her last relationship didn't end well. And she's given herself a full year to get her head on straight. Now she's hoping for a fresh start and she's ready to start dating again. She wonders what kind of man she'll find this time.

She's attractive. She has dark brown curly hair. Her honey brown eyes sometimes turn hazel green. She's a very happy person. She loves to laugh and when she does her eyes sparkle and you can see the dimples in her cheeks. The dimples give her a sort of cuteness.

Her background is Russian. But she's been taken for other nationalities; Italian, Spanish, Latina, Egyptian, and mixed race African American. She's been told by voice coaches that she has a polyglot accent; when she talks no one can figure out where she's from based on her speech alone. If life had turned out differently for her, she might have made a great news personality. Her looks would appeal to a diverse audience.

She has certain energy about her. When she walks into a room, men turn and look at her. She knows how to reflect that energy back at them. She smiles a lot and she makes eye contact. It makes her seem friendly and approachable. Men interpret it as a feeling that she's interested in them. She loves men and they love her. And men love her body. She catches them looking at her, especially at her breasts and her legs. It's been that way for as long as she can remember. A lot of the men she meets have a look in their eyes that tells her they want to fuck her. She knows it, loves it, and uses it. After all, just because they want it, doesn't mean that they'll get it. She's been told that she has the "3 B's." She's beautiful, brainy, and buxom." It's a winning combination with men.

Intelligence turns her on. So does deep conversation with an open minded, good looking man. She doesn't really have a type, but she seems to gravitate toward men with dark hair and green eyes. And the man has to be taller than she is. Being with someone taller makes her feel protected. And in bed it helps her feel dominated.

She's a Gemini, sun sign of the twins. And like the twins, she's full of contradiction and duality. She's serious and silly. She's rational, but often acts on instinct alone. She's very feminine, but engages in some masculine behaviors. At times, she's aggressive, but she can also be provocatively shy. She's highly educated, but often gravitates toward those who aren't. She's outgoing, but has long periods of intense self-reflection. She can be tough as nails, but cries when someone hurts her feelings.

She's an excellent communicator. She can see both sides of a situation and communicate her observations extremely well. It's no wonder she became a trial lawyer. She can paint a vivid picture with her words. Her mind is fast and clever. And she's always thirsting for knowledge that she wants to share with others. She's enthusiastic about life, but becomes easily bored with dull people and routines. It's a good thing for her that she found a dynamic career that keeps her constantly working on different cases and puts her in a courtroom. She can't be chained to a desk.

She's completely uninhibited. She enjoys sex and enjoys pleasing her partner. She's decisive, in her life and in bed. She's creative, playful, and thoughtful. Her thoughtfulness is in gaining an understanding of her sex partner. She listens, observes, and remembers things extremely well.

Sara likes to plan. She can choreograph a sexual encounter like the dance routines she once performed. The energy is all hers. Her lovers just go along with it. At first, they like it. They're attracted to her wildness. But with rare exception, her experience is that they wind up wanting to possess and change her. The truth is that just like the element of air attached to her Gemini sign; she's a free spirit. She's like a bird you set free that keeps coming back to you. She won't let you put her in a cage.

At the urging of a girlfriend, she sets up a profile on the dating site *OK Cupid*. This is her first foray into the world of online dating. Her friend gives her some advice: "First, make sure that you're the only person in your pictures and include a full body shot. Second, don't say anything negative in your profile. Last, you have to be the one to approach the men, because most of them will be too insecure to approach you." That last part bothers Sara. She craves someone who's dominant and aggressive, at least in bed. If a man is too insecure to approach her, how will he be able to give her what she needs?

When Sara tells another girlfriend, a colleague at work, about her plans to go on an Internet dating site, she warns her to be careful. "Don't give out your real name. Make up a name for your profile. Don't tell anyone exactly where you live. If you decide to meet someone, meet him in a public place like a Starbucks. And make sure he doesn't follow you home when you leave. And don't give him your phone number. Ask him for his number first."

The tips from her friend sound like good advice. But Sara is going it to take it a step further. She plans to do a little investigating before she agrees to meet anyone in person. All she really needs is three pieces of personal information to confirm that a man she meets online is who he claims to be. For example, if she knows his first name, the city where he lives or works, and his line of work, she'll find him through the Internet. And when she locates him she'll know, because the picture from OKC will match the one on social media, like Facebook or LinkedIn or on a business website.

Sara decides that her dating site name will be "Mia." She thinks that her profile should sound positive, engaging, playful, and a little sexy. She doesn't want to attract perverts or men that just want a hook up. But she doesn't want Mr. Plain Vanilla either. She's hoping to find a man with whom she can have a long-term relationship. Sara writes a short profile. It reads:

It's hard to describe yourself in a few lines, but here goes. I'm positive and optimistic. I believe that life is what you make of it. I try to always stay focused on the present and not worry about the future. I make a conscious effort not to be critical of others. I try to live in a state of gratitude. I'm an educated professional. I work hard and try to play hard. I enjoy a very healthy life style. I exercise every day, eat right, and try to limit stress as much as possible. I enjoy looking my best. High heels are a must! I'm affectionate and compassionate. My friends would describe me as intelligent, confident, sexy, kind, trustworthy, hardworking, accomplished, and goal oriented. What do men notice about me? My eyes, my smile, and my curves.

She only posts one picture; a head shot taken when she was in the Caribbean. She answers some of the platform's "matching" questions that don't seem too personal for public view, such as: Are you a cat person or a dog person? *Dog.* How much can intelligence turn you on? *A lot.* Is astrological sign at all important in a match? *Yes.* Can you cook? *Yes.* Do you enjoy discussing politics? *Yes.* Could you date someone who does drugs? *No.* Do you believe in karma? *Yes.*

She also provides other information, such as her favorite movies; pretty much anything with Tom Hanks, Leonardo DiCaprio or Amy Adams. She decides not to mention things that won't appeal to men. For example, that one of her favorite TV shows is Wendy Williams or that she has a secret celebrity crush on Josh Groban. In fact, she'd be happy if she meets someone who resembles him somewhat.

Sara's never been involved with anyone younger than her. She sets the age preference option, which will also appear on her profile page, to 50 – 65. In just under two weeks, she has over 200 likes from men who view her profile. And those two weeks bring a variety of men sending messages. Most of the messages say something like, "Hi. I like your profile. How are you?" The men who are a bit more creative mention something about her appearance, "You have amazing eyes" or "a great smile." Or they comment on something they like in her self-description or mention something they think they have in common with her.

She also receives messages from a variety of disingenuous and otherwise strange people. Some men are dishonest about their age and are way too old for her. The profile might say that a man is 55. But in the pictures, he looks to be at least 80. Some men are less than truthful about their current circumstances. A man from the UK messages Sara and says that the distance won't be an impediment to a relationship with him. He doesn't mention that he's currently incarcerated. His profile picture shows that he is behind bars in a prison cell. Then there are the men with fetishes. One man wants to worship her feet. He wants to know if she's willing to paint her toe nails red and wear an ankle bracelet and toe rings. Some men just want sex and are graphic in expressing their desires. Like the guy who wants to know if Sara is interested in dating him and his friend at the same time. She replies, "Say what?" The man responds that he wants to fuck her while she's on top of him while his friend is behind her fucking her in the ass. She hits the delete button after reading that one.

Some of the men are on active military duty and deployed, living in extreme danger. They seem to be looking for the distraction of a conversation. Then there are imposters; people who likely appropriate a picture of a good looking man and set up a fake profile page. For a while Sara thought she was talking with a general who lived in DC. When she started asking him innocuous questions about his background he became non-responsive. Then his profile page suddenly disappeared. Using her investigative skills, she tracked down the person in the photograph through resources on the Internet. The real person whose picture was used is married and lives in Florida. She figures that the profile pages with scant information, few or no matching questions answered, and photos of an unusually attractive man are fakes. The person behind the fabricated identity might be a con artist looking for lonely hearts to defraud. Or it may be a Catfish; a man using a fictional online persona who's lonely, bored, curious or married trying to trick someone into a relationship.

Some of the men have very sad lives. There are widowers trying to raise children alone who are looking for a woman to be a mother for the family. Others were dealing with serious health issues or have suffered terrible loss. Most women might simply ignore their messages. But Sara has a kind heart. She sends them back a message saying something like, "Thanks for your kind note. Sorry to hear that you're dealing with such a difficult situation. I looked at your profile. Unfortunately, I don't think we'd be a good match. But I wish you all the best in your search. I hope you find a great woman." You can tell from the replies to her messages that these men are happy just to be acknowledged.

After viewing numerous profiles, Sara comes to a conclusion about the men overall. Generally, men over age 50 are not attractive to her. A lot of them are overweight and don't look healthy. She leads a very healthy, active life style and is hoping to find someone who's like-minded. At the other end of the spectrum, there are men on the site who are body builders or triathletes. But she isn't interested in connecting with a man who wants to spend 4 hours a day in the gym. Most of the men are bald or if they have hair, it's generally white or grey – which makes them look even older. She goes back into the platform settings and lowers her bottom acceptable age to 45. She figures that at least it will be fun to look at younger men.

Sara goes on two dates. The first date is lunch with a good looking widower in his mid-50s. Unfortunately, he talks for a full hour about his dead wife and how she never wanted to spend any time with him. He doesn't ask Sara a single question about herself. The next morning, she realizes that when they left the restaurant, he immediately texted her the message, "Had a great time. See you again?" *Unbelievable.* The other man was a little younger and had hair. He was an actuary. He was so boring and dull Sara thought she might actually fall asleep while he was speaking. Afterwards, he texted her a message asking, "Do you like to kiss?" *Are we in 6th grade? I do like to kiss, but I'm not kissing you.* Each of these men wanted to kiss Sara at the end of their date. But as they leaned near her, Sara quickly extended her hand, saying, "It was really nice to meet you." All she would give them was a handshake. Honestly, after those two encounters she was starting to doubt the whole online dating thing.

When she reads a message received from 34-year old Declan, she laughs out loud. He says:

"Hey there! I'm Declan, how's it going today?"

The picture that appears along with his message shows a cute, young, dark haired man playing a guitar. At first, she assumes he hasn't noticed her age on the profile page. Maybe he only noticed her picture. She looks younger than she is. The conversation goes this way:

S: "You're so cute. But way too young for me. Have a good day!"

D: "I'm so sad I'm too young for you! It's unfortunate because you're quite cute yourself! And very sexy... I really think you should give me a chance despite my age. :)"

S: "OK. So just out of complete curiosity, what do you think we would have in common?"

D: "Well, at the very least I think we have mutual attraction in common. The rest we could probably find out by way of some nice pillow talk. :)"

S: "That's what I figured. I'm sorry, but I think I'd feel like I was robbing the cradle. And I'm really not looking for a hook up. I'm hoping to find a long-term relationship. But good luck. I'm sure you'll find someone great."

D: "I'm definitely disappointed. And just so it's out there, I would never dream of treating a woman like you to one wonderful meeting, rather I'd hope for as many as we can."

S: "Thank you. You're very sweet."

D: "And you can trust that I'm a much older soul than my age indicates."

S: "I'm sure that's true. But why would you want to be with someone much older when you could be with a gorgeous young woman?"

D: "And your age is immaterial to me. I just find you extremely sexy and would love to charm my way into your bed, direct as that may be, but I prefer being up front. Younger women don't really do anything for me. I've always dated older. Starting back in college when I was in a fairly exciting affair with a professor. And you're an especially gorgeous woman yourself. I would be lucky to get to be with you. Is it completely out of the question for you? If so I will leave you be."

Sara leans back in her chair, looks at the computer screen, and thinks.

S: "I may just keep you in mind. But it would be against my better judgment."
D: "Well I certainly understand your trepidation, but I may have a certain.... asset that could help you decide."
S: "Really? What would that be?"
D: "An absolutely impressive endowment. If that sort of thing interests you at all. But by just talking about it I fear I'm blowing my chances."
S: "Thanks for the disclosure. I'll keep it and you in mind :)"
D: "I would love if you kept me more than just in your mind! Would you like my number?"
S: "You're persistent. I'll give you that. OK. And what's your name again?"
D: "My name is Declan. Text me at (202) 997-XXXX. I'll be looking forward to hearing from you! And getting to talk with a woman as attractive as you gives me plenty of reason to be so persistent! Also if you text me tonight I will have to get back to you in the morning. Took a dinner break and heading back in for work now! Have a lovely evening."
S: "You too, Declan. Sara"

Sara sits back from her computer screen. *What the hell just happened? I must be out of my fucking mind. How did he just mange to get his foot in the door?* Whatever it is, this younger man stirs something in her. She feels like a giant magnet is pulling her from across the room. *I'm not having a mid-life crisis, definitely not.* She's already been through that when at age 45 she impulsively bought a BMW convertible. This feels very different.

But what would any kind of relationship with this guy be? There's no possibility of anything lasting outside of a possible friendship. No demands, no expectations, just sex. That might be fine. But then she wonders if this man would really find her attractive in real time. She has a nice, curvy body. Her legs are toned from years of dance classes, endless miles on the exercise bike, and the luck of good genes. She's not a Barbie Doll, but she's in good shape. She figures that if they meet and there's no chemistry, she'll be in no worse a position.

Sara likes the name Declan, because it's unusual. She's learned just a little bit about him through his messages. He says that he's an old soul. Because he approached her, she hadn't read his profile. When she does read it, she's a little stunned. He sounds like your basic nice guy. But it strikes her that he has unusual taste in music for someone his age. He likes music from the 60's and 70's and Blues. His profile also says that he plays harmonica and has a tattoo. *Lord, I hope he didn't learn to play harmonica and get that tattoo while spending time in prison. And I hope the tattoo isn't a picture of his Mother.* He wants to be like Indiana Jones. He has a demanding job, but doesn't define himself by his work. He's well-read and listens to NPR. Sara is intrigued by his background. This guy also loves animals, likes to play Scrabble, and admits that he cries at movies. *How can you not love this guy?*

She already has an idea of him. Of course, it could be completely wrong. She doesn't even know this man, hasn't even laid her eyes on him. She always tries to resist drawing conclusions about situations without having all the facts. She's learned through her work and in her personal life that a single piece of information can completely change your perspective about almost anything. But she thinks from the information she has, including his unusual profile name, that he's creative, open-minded, and curious. He's a non-conformist. She wonders if he might enjoy her being sexually aggressive with him. He's potentially a passionate friend. He's the kind of guy who seems cool on the outside, but might be emotional inside. He's a free-spirit, like her. If that's true, in bed, he'll likely do whatever she wants to excite and please her. Like music, they'll dance together in a long overture before engaging in sex. She hopes that he doesn't get lost in sexual fantasy, wasting time masturbating when instead, he could be fucking her.

Sara knows one thing for certain about this situation. She needs to be very careful how she thinks about Declan. When a man gives a woman sensations she's never experienced before, she can easily fall in love with him. If this evolves into any kind of relationship, she realizes that it automatically comes with an expiration date. But no one really knows what the future holds. And she likes to stay focused on the present.

There's nothing in his profile to suggest his interest in older women. Except that he says the age range he's looking for is 20 to 50. But Sara notices that most everyone on this dating platform lists a wide age range of interest. However, she's not just older then Declan. She's almost 20 years his senior. There was nothing to suggest that any kind of relationship would work with this man. There was nothing to warn what was about to happen. Little did she know that behind the cute, mundane profile was a lion.

CHAPTER 2

Texting is Talking,
Sexting is Much More

• • •

Day 1

S: "Hi Declan, What kind of work do you do that you are at the office so late at night?"

D: "I work on IT security for a large International corporation. We do most of our business in China and they're 12 hours ahead. Hence my odd schedule."

S: "Are you exhausted? I was wondering if you work in a bar."

D: "Haha, I wish. I'm a bit tired but not too bad. What are you up to today?"

S: "Just some work. After I finish, I'm going to take the dog for a walk. There's a great path not far from the house."

D: "Very nice! Sounds quiet relaxing. I took my dog out for a long walk this morning. I have to say I'm really glad I finally convinced you."

S: "Well, so far you've convinced me to get to know you. LOL. What kind of a dog do you have?"

Declan sends Sara a picture of a beautiful chocolate Lab, sitting in a desk chair.

D: "What about you?"

S: "He's beautiful. My phone is messed up so I can't send a pic from here. But my dog is a super adorable, black and tan poodle mix. And he's the friendliest ever – he's a Velcro dog. I also have a 10 year old cat. The poor guy had dental surgery yesterday and they gave him a multi-day pain killer. So he's loopy. That's why I'm home today. Otherwise, I'd be at my office in D.C."

D: "Ah Gotcha. So what do you do?"

S: "I'm a trial attorney."

D: "Admirable work!"

S: "Thank you. How long have you lived in this area?"

D: "About 4 years. But my company moves people around. I'm about due for a transfer."

S: "So, I'll get to liking you and then you'll get sent some place far away…"

D: "An unfortunate possibility. It's part of why I try to keep things – and I hate to use this word – more casual."

S: "I'm just teasing you. Do your friends know about your interest in older women?"

D: "Nope. But they do sometimes openly wonder why I don't date the women at work. I just say that I don't dip the pen in company ink."

S: "You're funny. If you worked so late why aren't you sleeping? Aren't you tired?"

D: "Well, I am lying in bed. But the construction outside is making an awful racket."

S: "It does seem like something is always being built in DC these days. How does your schedule work?

D: "It's sort of chaotic. I get stretched pretty thin. I'm going to try to get some ZZs before going back to the office. Hope you have a wonderful evening, gorgeous :)"

DAY 2

D: "Good morning! How was your night?"

S: "It was alright. How was work last night?"

D: "It was good."

S: "Hey, do you have a pic of yourself that you can please send me? The ones you have on OKC all have other people with you."

Declan texts Sara a picture of himself. In the picture, he's wearing a suit and tie. She thinks he's very good looking; he's handsome. He vaguely reminds her of her college boyfriend. Her mind drifts for a moment recalling where she was in life in her early 30's. She remembers that she was working for the District Attorney, prosecuting murder cases. *I was an adult by that point, certainly not a child.*

S: "Thank you. I've been thinking about you. But I don't have a lot to go on. Tell me something about yourself please."

D: "How do you mean? I'm a computer security expert and a musician. I have a PhD in Computer Science."

S: "You're awesome. What kind of music do you like? What instrument do you play?"

D: "I play guitar and harmonica. Love blues, huge fan of Buddy Guy and Stevie Ray. Mostly though, I listen to a lot of Beatles and Led Zep. The rest I'd like to tell you following our consummation. If that suits you. And thank you for the compliment. I think you'll find I don't take kind words very easily for some reason."

S: "Consummation? That sounds so serious and final. I was thinking more like wild, break the furniture sex. LOL. Your taste in music does reflect an old soul. Mustang Sally and all. It's great music. I'm studying piano. I've only been playing a few months, but have always loved music. And I'm being serious about it. I have a great teacher and I practice every day. I also sing in a choir."

D: "And yes, I was hoping for wild and crazy sex, but I was going to leave that ball in your court. And that's awesome! Piano is such a fun instrument. I can play a little bit, but I'm not used to reading piano music so it takes me a bit. I tend to pick out melodies on my keyboard and translate them to guitar. You've got me quite aroused at the moment, by the way."

S: "If that's all it takes to get you aroused I might do you in when we're together."

D: "It is easy to arouse me. I'm currently standing quite solidly at attention due to you. I would LOVE to see more of you."

S: "What time do you have to leave for work?"

D: "I could talk later today, sure. If you're available around 3 we could talk a bit. I am way too tempted to show you a picture of my current distraction."

S: "That sounds good. Please give me a call when you're ready. And maybe we'll see each other sometime. Though I feel as if I'm about to take a bite from forbidden fruit. I don't think I can resist."

D: "It's the sweetest of fruits. When are you typically free, maybe on a Friday? And I trust that if I send you a picture that you'll keep it to yourself. And that you're not under age. Would you like to see?"

S: "Sure."

Sara didn't realize what Declan was referring to as his "current distraction." Declan texts Sara a picture of his cock. She gasps when she looks at it. It is the biggest one she's ever seen. *Maybe he just clipped this picture from the Internet to shock me. This can't be real. But what if it is?*

S: "Oh my! You weren't exaggerating."

D: "And that's not even a very good angle :) I can't get a dollar bill all the way around it. Would it be possible to see more of you? Doesn't have to be naughty unless you want it to be."

S: "I'd love to tease you, but I just can't send those kinds of pics. Possible future employment and all."

D: "I do understand."

S: "You've got me so I'm not really thinking straight. And I'm not even going got ask the reason it occurred to you to try the dollar bill thing. I've never contemplated cash as a unit of measure in that way. I've got to get back into work mode, somehow. Talk to you later."

D: "I figure it gives a good idea of thickness. Something you can easily reference yourself. But you have a good and productive day. I'll try to talk to you later."

S: "Just so you know, I'm having an impossibly hard time concentrating today. You've driven me to distraction. What will I do with you?"

Declan didn't call Sara that day. She figured that he must have slept through his alarm and had been late for work. The next day she sent him a text. When he didn't reply, it occurred to her that she might never hear from him again. She tried to put him out of her mind, but failed. Unbelievably, he was all she was thinking about.

DAY 3

S: "Declan, Are you OK?"

DAY 4

D: "Hey! So sorry about that yesterday, wound up sleeping through the alarm and racing back to the office."

S: "No worries. I thought that was what happened. But, it did occur to me that you might not be real. Maybe just a bored married guy looking for some stimulation. I was hoping I was wrong. I'm enjoying your intellect and our sexual banter."

D: "Nah, still single. Largely because my life is so hectic. NO time to be bored! How are you doing this morning?"

S: "Fine thanks. I had a girlfriend from high school days passing through town and I invited her to stay over last night. She left this morning."

D: "Did you just hang out and chat?"

S: "Yes and she remembered things we did together that I'd forgotten. Like the time my Dad took our family to stay on a Dairy farm in PA. I guess he thought it would be a good learning experience. I convinced my friend to come along. She was a good sport. What do you like to do for exercise?"

D: "Mostly I run and lift. Though I've dropped off my running a bit to only 9 miles a week, used to do 15. What about you?"

S: "That's impressive. I wish I could run. My body type doesn't make it conducive. So, I do the bike, elliptical, and weights."

D: "Yeah, that's why I dialed back my running. I was doing more damage than good at that rate. My knees are suffering the results."

S: "That's no good. You need your knees. Mine don't bother me. How tall are you?"

D: "I'm 5'7". What's your reason for not running?"

S: "You're not the only one who is well endowed, Sir. 36DD over here. I hope you like that :)"

D: "I do…so very much."

D: "Now here I am running errands with gradually tightening pants."

S: "Sorry about that, but please know that I'd be very happy to take care of your problem. It's a shame you aren't here with me."

D: "I wish I was. Are you at home?"

S: "Yes. Presently on the Life Cycle. Or at least trying to be through this very pleasant distraction."

D: "What are you wearing?"

S: "I could make something up to excite you more. But honestly, just skin tight yoga shorts and a T-shirt."

D: "That's plenty exciting for me."

D: "I would love so much to see…"

S: "I'm hoping that the chemistry in person is as hot as I feel it remotely. I hope it's not just some fantasy in my head. I do have that creative energy thing going. It can get me into trouble if I'm not careful."

D: "I'm sure it will be. A gorgeous, curvy woman like you will send me into a fever."

S: "And I'd like to oblige. But not feeling camera ready at the moment. LOL."

D: "Oh don't worry about that. You're going to look like you've been working out when we are done anyway."

D: "I'm getting all hot and bothered thinking about you pumping away on that bike."

S: "I guess we should get together then. But wouldn't I be insane to invite a man I really don't know into my house, into my bed? You're a stranger to me."

D: "I can definitely understand why you might be reticent, but at the same time I think that both our juices are flowing and the passion will be overwhelming should we meet."

S: "Yes."

D: "I'm having a hard time not touching myself at the moment."

S: "Me too. And I've been having some great fantasies about you. If I wasn't so thoroughly schooled in Stranger Danger I might be tempted to give you my address and the code to the front door right now."

D: "And I'd hope to find you naked in bed waiting for me. Tell me about your other fantasies. I would love to fulfill one for you."

S: "I think that just by being here you will."

D: "I just might come over to you now."

S: "Don't you have to work later?"

D: "Yes, but there are things I will sacrifice for a beautiful woman."

D: "Especially one with whom I have such sexual chemistry."

S: "I like that. Thank you. Maybe we can get together. If you've been trying to get under my skin you've succeeded."

D: "I'm trying to get under that T-shirt you're wearing..."

S: "I'm hoping to bring you a little shock and awe when you see..."

D: "No teasing to slake my thirst for your body?"

He just used the words "reticent" and "slake." I'm never playing Scrabble with him.

S: "Are you thirsty?"

D: "When it comes to you I'm parched, yearning."

S: "You're driving me crazy."

D: "I'm sitting in my car rubbing my self through my pants because I can't stop thinking about you."

Declan texts Sara a picture of his hard-on pushing through his pants.

S: "Wish I could do that for you. Wow. I hope I can "accommodate" you."

D: "I'll go slow and easy until you're ready."

S: "My clit is throbbing."

D: "You should rub it a bit."

D: "Do you like having your breasts played with?"

S: "I think I need to put this phone down now. It's that or a cold shower."

D: "Keep playing with me!"

S: "Happy to. Tell me what you want to do to me?"

D: "That depends. What are you wearing when I come over?"

S: "What would you like me to wear? Maybe a skirt you could slide up when I face you and sit on your lap?"

D: "Mmmm, yes a skirt would be nice. And maybe something you don't have to wear a bra with? Though I'm not sure with your body if that's a feasible request."

D: "So you turn to me and throw one leg around me and straddle my lap, huh?"

D: "I wrap my arms around your waist and pull you in close to me, press our bodies together as I kiss you passionately and deeply."

D: "You feel my cock growing against you; you press your breasts into my face as you grind against my crotch."

D: "I slide your skirt up and you've decided to forego panties for our meeting."

D: "With one hand on the back of your neck pulling your face to mine, our tongues entangle as I reach down with my free hand and explore the skin inside your thighs."

D: "I feel the warmth and wetness of your pussy growing. I slip your top off and your large breasts fall toward me. I reach and bring one up to my face and begin kissing and sucking as I slide my fingers between the lips of your pussy."

D: "Suddenly, I throw you down off of me onto your back on the couch. Your breasts and pussy fully exposed. I can't help myself. I grab your legs and spread them apart as I bring my tongue to the lips of your pussy."

D: "Would you like me to stop? Did you cum for me?"

S: "Not yet. Keep going."

D: "I start to lick up and down between your lips. One hand reaches up and firmly grabs one of your breasts while with the other hand I begin to penetrate you. Just slowly working my fingers in and out as my tongue finds your clit."

D: "When you're close to climaxing I stop and kneel between your legs."

D: "I slide my throbbing hard cock out of my pants and lean over you, the tip of my cock hovering just outside your pussy."

D: "I slide the tip up and down between your lips, getting it nice and wet. You moan and roll your eyes back, practically begging for me to thrust into you."

S: "Lord have mercy."

D: "Our lips lock as I firmly but slowly penetrate you with my cock."

D: "You moan into my mouth in pleasure."

D: "You feel my cock pumping into you over and over."

D: "You begin cumming. The feeling of your pussy squeezing me as I thrust brings me to the edge."

S: "I don't even know what to say. You leave me speechless and yearning. So hot."

D: "I just want to see what you look like right now. In the throes of ecstasy, pussy wet and wanting."

D: "My cock is so hard for you right now."

S: "I want to feel your lips pressed against mine, your tongue in my mouth. And your body next to mine."

D: "Inside you…"

S: "We have to stop. Sadly, I have a business lunch today with all men. I need to get ready. I know they will see that something is up with me. The thought of you brings a mischievous smile to my face. And then there is the pheromone thing. I have to get into business serious mode. Thank you for a delightful morning. I'll send you some possible dates we can see each other shortly."

D: "Please do. I can't wait to see you."

S: "And I you."

D: "And you should send me more than just dates. I would love some selfies from you :)"

S: "I may send you something later today. I'm about to head out the door. I'm curious about your background. I hope you don't mind me asking. I'm mostly Russian."

D: "I'm mostly Austrian, 1/8th Irish. And I can't wait to see what you send me. My cock is constantly throbbing for you."

S: "Austrian. I think you're the first Austrian man I've ever met. I'm going to have to do some research."

D: "Oh yeah? About what?"

Sara doesn't answer his question. She goes to Google and enters "Characteristics of Austrian men" into the search box to see what pops up. Declan and Sara have a brief phone call just before Sara's meeting. She loves his voice. After the call, the texting starts again.

D: "God that was sexy. I know your sitting there with all those men and the idea that your mind is on me and my fat, throbbing cock while you try to suppress the arousal is turning me on so much."

S: "Are you trying to torture me? You take my breath away. So thank you for the exquisite agony. The anticipation of having you is driving me mad."

S: "I'm glad that you are aroused by the thought that while I'm in the company of other men my mind is on you."

D: "Would you like to see what happens when I think about it?"

S: "Yes, I would."

D: "First, tell me about how you want me to take you the first time."

S: "I want to feel you on top of me in my bed. Then I want you in between my legs. I can't wait to wrap my legs around you and feel you touching my body. I'm tight and you'll have to force yourself in me somewhat. But I know I'll be begging you to keep going even though I might feel as though I can't take it."

Declan texts Sara another picture of his cock taken from a different angle. It looks even larger than in the earlier photo.

S: "OMG! I'll send you a pic later today. Bye."

S: "Also, I have a question for you. On a scale of 1 to 10, with 1 being plain vanilla and 10 being violent BDSM, where would you put yourself?"

The next day, Sara texts Declan a picture of herself. She's wearing a black sweater open in the front. Her ample cleavage is on full display in a black lace bra. Her face is not seen.

Day – 5

D: "Good morning lovely."

S: "Good morning. Did you receive the pic I sent you this morning?"

D: "Yes, I was just looking at it."

S: "Did you think about me last night?"

D: "I did…"

D: "Several times I had to stop what I was doing while thinking about you."

S: "Tell me what you were thinking."

D: "I was thinking about exploring your luscious body with my hands."

D: "Feeling my way around your skin with my lips."

D: "Working your clothes off slowly and sensually while you straddle me."

S: "I will eagerly anticipate your touch. But don't you want a taste?"

D: "Of course I do. I want to taste your soft skin until your pussy is warm and wet and waiting for my tongue."

D: "What are you doing today?"

S: "I have a meeting with lawyers. Why? Do you want me right now? I woke up in the middle of the night. I was so hot and ready thinking about you. I was tempted to call you and beg you to come to me."

D: "Of course I want you right now. I want you always."

D: "My cock is so hard for you anytime I even think about you."

S: "I feel like I will explode. I want to come in your mouth. Then taste it on your lips."

D: "Oh dear god yes. Straddle my face and let me lick you."

D: "I want to see your full breasts bouncing as I drive my cock into you over and over again."

S: "I don't want to be selfish. Maybe I can suck your cock at the same time. Or maybe you would prefer me on my knees naked in front of you so you can see your huge self going in and out of my mouth as I tease you without mercy."

S: "I hope you know I can keep this up forever..."

D: "I hope you can. Because as long as you can keep it up I want to be your boy toy and take part."

Declan texts Sara another pic of his cock. His face is in the picture this time. The photos are genuine. His cock is enormous.

S: "Wow. When I see you erect and throbbing I just want you again and again. And this crazy thought runs through my mind, "Objects are larger than they appear in the mirror." LOL."

D: "Are you working out right now?"

S: "Love it. And yes, I did the bike and I'm on the Elliptical. Or at least trying to be. You make it hard, Baby."

D: "You should take a break and slide those yoga pants down."

S: "I intend to do just that. Maybe you would like to watch sometime. I'd be happy to put on a show for you."

D: "I would absolutely love to watch..."

D: "Is there any way you can video chat with your phone?"

S: "I'm not sure I want to do that yet. I don't want anything that might lessen the impact the first time I see you and we touch."

S: "And you are going to ruin me for other men."

D: "That's of course not my goal but I am more than happy to show you the pleasures of a big, hard cock bringing you to orgasm."

S: "Thank you."

D: "I just want to make you cum over and over again."

S: "And I hope that if you are my boy toy you will also be my friend. I can't just have you in a box in my mind marked "sex.""

D: "Of course I will be! Can't be a friend with benefits without being friends!"

S: :)

D: "Can't promise I won't be undressing you with my eyes every time we meet though."

D: "And my cock won't engorge and throb at your presence."

D: "And that the very sound of your voice won't send me into lustful passion."

D: "Which is to say that should we go out for coffee or be in a social setting I would likely try to slyly slide my fingers into your wet and waiting pussy."

S: "And I would absolutely let you do that. You don't really know how wild I can be. I never thought of myself as a cougar. But I'm definitely a tiger."

D: "And I will do everything in my power to encourage that animalistic side of you."

D: "You asked me a question a while ago that I forgot to answer: on a scale of 1 to 10 vanilla – BDSM I'm probably an 8."

S: "What a happy coincidence. That would be me too. You might want to put on your seat belt. I think we could be in for quite a ride."

D: "Would you be on the more dominant or submissive side?"

S: "I've studied it like a science. I think I would qualify for a Master's Degree. No pun intended. I'm not into the violence, but I love the dynamics. And we are consenting adults."

S: "To answer your question, I could be either. However, although I like to drive, mostly I love to be driven. If that gives you a hint."

S: "And you?"

D: "I can definitely accommodate that. I've got some pretty crazy desires. I mostly identify as a hedonist and love to bring pleasure for others."

S: "I like that. You'll have to excuse me now. I have a date with my shower massager, who I will need to name Steve if I don't get some relief from you soon. Talk to you later."

D: "Steve?"

S: "Would you prefer "Declan?""

D: "Maybe only if you share some pictures of "Declan" at work."

Men are so damn visual.

D: "I have a lot of very dirty desires when it comes to you."

S: "Your wish is my command, but I'm a little worried about electric shock from an iPhone in the shower. LOL."

D: "Hahaha, well don't do anything dangerous. But please do get naughty for me."

S: "With pleasure…I hope you'll be picturing it in your mind. While I'm doing that, I'll be thinking about you pounding into me."

D: "So tell me some of your more perverse desires."

S: "I will probably have to whisper them into your ear. It makes me feel a little shy and embarrassed to ask you to do something that has only been a fantasy, at least until now."

D: "You shouldn't be. You're sharing your desires with your future lover."

S: "You better stop or I might fall in love with you."

D: "Share and let me know the thoughts and ideas that really turn you on."

S: "I don't want to tell you everything all at once. But there's one idea. I'd like to put oil on my body and have you on top of me sliding your thick cock in between my breasts."

D: "Mmmmm that might make me cum pretty quick with those big breasts of yours."

S: "I won't let you. I just want to see and feel you doing that."

D: "When we are together, where do you want me to cum?"

S: "In my mouth or on me. Is that OK?"

D: "That is more than OK."

S: "Do you think you can cum more than once with me?"

D: "I know for a fact that I will."

S: "I'll love that. I can almost climax just thinking about you and anticipating what's coming. I think I'm good for 5-6 times with you."

S: "You have the biggest cock I've ever seen in my life. I hope I can handle it. And you."

D: "Just dropped the phone..."

Declan and Sara make plans for him to come to her house the next day, which is Valentine's Day. Before Sara will give him her address she asks for his last name and the name of the company where he works. He gives her both. She might be foolish about inviting him to her home, but she's not stupid. She plans to verify his identity and see what she can learn about him, before she lets him in the door. Within a minute, she finds him on Facebook and on the website for his company.

D: "What do you enjoy sexually?"

S: "How do you mean?"

D: "I guess I should ask more pointedly, are there any no-go areas?"

S: "Whatever you want is fine. Anything you want, as long as you don't hurt me."

D: "Would never dream of it. Do you enjoy anal?"

S: "I haven't done that. Do you like to do that? Is that what you want to do to me?"

D: "I want to do it all to you."

D: "I want to fuck your ass while I play with you tits. Mmmm."

S: "What makes you think I would let you take control and dominate me like that?"

D: "Cause you have a thing for me, obviously."

D: "I think you would like to have someone else take control and make decisions for once after all you do at work."

S: "So what if I do? Doesn't mean you should own me."

D: "I don't own you."

S: "If I let you do whatever you want, you just might. LOL."

D: "Yes. You're gorgeous. I want to explore your body."

S: "What makes you so aggressive?"

S: "Whatever it is, you're making me ache to be submissive to you and feel you dominate me."

D: "You tell me when you want Daddy to come over."

S: "I'm completely on fire for you. We don't have to do everything all at once, do we?"

D: "Of course not. But I want this to be world shattering sex for you."

S: "I know it will be. Just being with you will be enough."

D: "I can't wait to feel that little pussy throbbing around my cock while you cum."

S: "I can't wait to have you inside me."

D: "I'm going to have to control myself. I'll be tempted to grab your hair, pull you down, and fuck you roughly from behind."

OMG! In that position, he'll be as deep inside me as possible.

S: "The idea of that excites me."
D: "Maybe flip you over and lock your knees against my shoulders while I thrust my cock into you, wrap one hand around your neck and squeeze?"

That's hot, but a little scary.

S: "What are you trying to do to me? I can barely function right now."
D: "I'm trying to make you touch yourself while you think about my fat cock driving into you."
S: "I'm in the grocery store. LOL."
D: "Find an empty aisle and touch yourself for a moment."
S: "There are cameras everywhere. Are you kidding? LOL."
D: "I'd love so much to meet you someplace public and get naughty with you."
S: "We can do that as long as we don't get arrested."
D: "See you tomorrow."

Unfortunately, Sara has a family emergency and she has to cancel the plans.

D: "It's too bad we can't have our play time."
S: "Yes, it is. But maybe it's better we're not together today. I have a feeling I would be left thinking of you every Valentine's Day for the rest of my life."
D: "Fair point."
S: "How are you today?"
D: "I'm alright. A bit sad that I'm not inside you at the moment."
S: "Me too. I might send you a pic later."

D: "Something to help me picture you more fully."

S: "Yes. I'd love to be your next wet dream."

D: "Well you were my last one so it would be appropriate."

S: "That makes me smile. What did you dream we were doing?"

D: "You, me and another woman."

D: "So… a lot."

S: "I think you're very dangerous for me. Is this a fantasy or something you want to do with me?"

D: "It is most definitely both."

S: "Oh mercy. I can't tell you all of my secrets before we meet."

D: "Now you HAVE to tell me!"

S: "I guess the cat will have to be out of the bag now. I'm bi. But I fight not to act on it. And I've been successful for quite a while. I want to be with a man. The women I've been with fall in love. Some have been a little crazy about it. The kind of woman you'd want us to be with would likely be more interested in your huge cock. I think I might feel jealous watching you kiss and fuck another woman. Or at least at this point in time."

D: "The thought of you with another woman just made my cock that much bigger…

No surprise here. This is every man's fantasy.

S: "That doesn't seem possible. If it excites you to think about it, I'm glad. I wasn't planning to tell you for fear it might turn you off."

D: "Literally my fantasy."

I was right.

S: "I'll keep that in mind. Please keep it our secret."

D: "Yes ma'am."

D: "When was the last time you were with a woman?"

S: "I would be willing to tell you stories when we're together if that would excite you to fuck me harder."

S: "Although I am looking forward to seeing your green eyes."

S: "They are green, right?"

D: "How'd you know?"

S: "Lucky guess."

S: "Anyway, can't stop thinking about you taking me from behind. Huge turn on. I'm so wet now just thinking about that."

D: "Fuck, you've already got me stroking my cock again."

S: "I'd like to do that for you."

D: "Do you finger yourself when you look at the pictures of my cock?"

S: "I'm waiting for you to penetrate me."

S: "I'm in the gym right now. Even with masturbating multiple times a day thinking about you, I have so much energy I have to do double workouts for longer. My body says to thank you."

D: "I'm sure your body will find a way to thank me..."

S: "Absolutely, repeatedly, and in every way I can imagine you would enjoy."

D: "My fantasy is, quite honestly, two curvaceous and insatiable older women."

D: "That's all I could ever want."

S: "Sadly, my taste in women is younger."

D: "How much younger?"

S: "Do you really want to know?"

D: "Very much so."

S: "It depends on the particular fantasy. Mine seem to revolve around power and control, or more accurately, the abuse thereof. So it depends if I'm the aggressor or the submissive."

D: "Please do tell me more while I stroke my cock to the thought."

S: "Well, if I was going to be the aggressor, I'd want someone inexperienced and more vulnerable without a point of reference whether I was being appropriate. It would take a woman with experience to truly dominate me and fuck me right."

S: "I know I'm so bad."

D: "You have no idea what kind of fantasy you'd be fulfilling for me."

Yes, I do.

D: "Seriously, it is impossible to find a woman like you."

S: "I'll take it under consideration and keep it in mind. For the time being, I'd really like to be your focus."

D: "You would be then. If we took control we would be using her for our pleasure."

S: "And I've never found a man like you either."

S: "I must admit, I'd love to watch a woman sucking your cock while I fuck her from behind with a strap-on dildo. That's such a hot image for me."

D: "Our eyes locked the entire time..."

D: "You lean in to kiss me as you thrust into her..."

S: "Yes. But I might have to look down from time to time and try not to cum too soon."

D: "I want to be fucking you from behind with her under you licking your pussy and my cock."

S: "Are you there yet, Baby? Can you cum for me?"

D: "I don't want to cum yet."

S: "And I can't wait to feel you shoot all over me."

S: "So you need more..."

D: "And I make her lick it off you."

D: "I want pictures."

D: "I want to see you in all your sexiness."

S: "Oh, I forgot to tell you the part where she is so overwhelmed by what is happening that she screams. I know I'm so twisted."

D: "I can make that happen quite easily with my cock."

S: "I can't wait. I think of you constantly. The thought of you wakes me up in the middle of the night. And I have to touch myself. But my old fantasies aren't working very well anymore, because I'm so filled with thoughts of you and the things we might do."

D: "What would you call me while we fuck?"

S: "Do you want to hear me calling your name? Or did you have a particular title that might excite you like Your Majesty, Master, or My Lord. LOL, but also curious."

D: "Anything that excites you and turns you on."

S: "I'll be saying, "Declan fuck me. Baby, do it harder. Please don't stop."

D: "Do you mostly cum from clitoral stimulation or from penetration?"

S: "Both. And I love both. I'm hoping you will want to suck my clit while you ram your fingers inside me, getting me ready to take all of your huge cock as deep as I can."

D: "Of course. Can I admit something dirty?"

S: "Of course, anything."

D: "I want you to be my mommy."

What the fuck? If he wants to wear a diaper and get inside a giant crib, I'm going to lose it.

S: "Really. Can you tell me exactly what you would want me to do?"

D: "I suppose just treat me like I'm your adult son, but incestuously."

Maybe I could just scream at him to go clean up his room.

D: "Is that something you might enjoy?"
S: "I think I'm going to have to get back to you on this one. I need a little time to wrap my mind around the idea."

Thank God I don't actually have a son.

S: "Who knows? Given our ages, I might feel maternal toward you from time to time. And I'm hoping that you'll be my Daddy on occasion. But with a completely different meaning. I'm sure you understand."
D: "Of course."
S: "If you give me what I need, I will try my best to do the same for you, Baby."
S: "I've had this funny thought. I meant to tell you about it earlier. You and I are out in public. We decide to go see a movie and we're waiting in line to buy tickets. The woman next to me in line looks at you and says, "Oh my, your son is so handsome." I glance at you and smile as I reply, "Yes, my son is very handsome." I turn toward you and say, "Baby, come give Mommy a great big kiss." So you step over to me, grab me, and begin to kiss me passionately, plunging your tongue into my mouth. It kind of goes south from there. People start freaking out, someone calls the police, and I get arrested. But they have to let me go once they figure out that you're well over the age of consent and we're just two deranged adults role playing our sexual fantasies. LOL."
D: "That's a really hot little thought."

Men really do only hear only what they want to hear.

S: Let's talk a little later. OK?
D: Sure.

Sara decides to do a little research. She turns to Google and queries, "Oedipus complex." Several sites pop up. She opens one and begins to read. The story is from Greek Mythology. Oedipus was left by his father on a mountain to die. But he was saved and raised by shepherds. He subsequently kills his father and marries his mother. The mother doesn't know when she marries him that Oedipus is her son or that he has killed her husband. When she learns the truth, she hangs herself and Oedipus blinds himself with pins from his mother's dress." *Wow. There's nothing erotic about that story.*

Next, Sara queries "mother son fantasies," and finds a treasure trove of incest porn stories. *How amazing. I had no idea. Google really is the best search engine.*

She gains a quick but comprehensive understanding of what these fantasies generally involve. It seems like the son in each story wants to get caught doing something naughty like masturbating on a pair of his Mom's panties, then the Mom gives in to lust and has sex with her son. *I had no idea about this. I'm going to have to be very creative to come up with a fantasy that Declan will love, and that I can tolerate.*

Sara realizes that she may need to negotiate with Declan about this line of fantasy. Of course, he won't know they're in actual negotiations. He'll just think they're talking about it so she can get accustomed to the idea. But Sara will know better.

There are three things Sara always does when she negotiates. First, she finds out everything she can about the other side, including what they really want out of the situation. *What's his real motivation here? What must he have to be happy with the outcome? Let's see, Declan wants to pretend he's having sex with his Mother. And he wants his Mother to want him, to enjoy the sex, and to be nurturing with him.* Second, you have to give the other side some of the things they want, but you don't necessarily have to give them everything. *So maybe I can be wearing a sexy apron and catch him in the act of doing something naughty like watching his Mother when he shouldn't be.* Third, make sure you get exactly what you want. *What do I really want? Oh yeah, to be fucked for as long and as hard as possible with that big cock. That shouldn't be a problem. But I'd really prefer he not constantly call me "Mommy" while he's fucking me.*

D: "Are you back?"

S: "Yes and you can relax. Everything you want is fine. The thought had already occurred to me given the difference in our age. Life is short. I told you I wasn't inhibited. As long as it's not illegal and doesn't involve children or animals, I will probably give you what you want. It's just words and what's in your head. I think everyone has dark fantasies. They just keep them secret. I have some I would never tell anyone."

S: "As for me, you'll be like an intoxicating drug in my body, my great escape from reality."

S: "Don't you need to sleep?"

D: "I'm a bit distracted."

S: "And by the way, I didn't ask you a reciprocal question. What would you call me in bed?"

D: "Maybe dirty slut, maybe Mommy. Depends on how you're acting."

S: "That's fine. As long as it's not in a child-like voice I think I can handle it."

D: "No. I'm your adult child. And you know about my huge cock and decided that you love me enough to act on your desires for me."

S: "Got it. I must say that this is a place I never envisioned going in fantasy land. But I'm willing to try it for you."

D: "Does it turn you on?"

S: "Well, you turn me on. That's all that matters for now. I really need to give this some thought. I think I need to see how it feels when we're together. I might need you to tell me one day where this comes from. I'm just curious. No pressure."

D: "It's just a fetish for the taboo."

Well there's a non-responsive answer if ever I've heard one.

S: "Understood. Any other disclosures I should know about now? You certainly know a lot about me."

D: "The idea of you pegging me turns me on."

I have no idea what he's talking about.

S: "Tell me."

D: "You would need to go slowly and easily and maybe with a small dildo. But I'm thinking about fucking another woman while you fuck me from behind."

What was it that Margaret Cho says about that? Oh yeah.

S: "You know that if I did that, you would never want to leave me, right?"

D: "I think that's already a true conclusion. I've never met a woman like you. You are everything I would love in a woman."

S: "What's your position on role play?"

D: "What are you going to wear?"

S: "You want costumes too?" LOL. "I'll see what I can do."

S: "I just hope that this is real. I know that I am."

D: "I hope so too."

D: "When I penetrate you will you tell me?"

S: "Yes. But I think I'll know when you hold me and kiss me."

S: "And if you don't get over here soon, I will hunt you down."

They make plans for Declan to come see Sara in about one week.

S: "Hey, what color nail polish do you like?"

D: "Hmmmm. Red? Something sultry."

S: "That's what I would have guessed. A nice contrast for my hands wrapped around your throbbing cock. Or my hands again the wall when you push me up against it to fuck me from behind."

D: "Would you ever be interested in swapping or sharing?"

S: "I don't think so. Not really my thing."

D: "You'd get too jealous you think?"

S: "I'm too concerned about disease and the lack of intimacy."

D: "Ahh yeah that makes sense."

S: "And also yes, I might feel jealous."

D: "I really love the idea of group sex."

S: "I'm not a jealous person though. I can tell you a story you might like."

S: "When I was in college, I had a boyfriend. You could say that I willingly walked through some doors with him that I shouldn't have."

S: "One of them was that he took me to a sex club in NYC. I was about 19 at the time. It was called, "Plato's Retreat." He didn't tell me where we were going. It was a surprise until we walked through the door."

D: "Wow. How did that go?"

S: "It was an interesting experience. I remember the place was underground. It had a dance floor and a swimming pool. There was also a large room where people were having sex and private rooms in the back. Pretty much everything you can imagine was going on."

D: "Not an experience you'd repeat I take it?"

S: "Well, that was before HIV. I would never want to take such a risk. And the experience changed me somewhat. I had planned to spend my life with that man. The fact that he was willing to allow another man to have me made me view him differently. I stopped seeing him as someone who could protect me. I need that perception."

D: "I see."

S: "But having sex with him while other people watched was a definite turn on. I found it extremely erotic. It was thrilling to know that people were getting aroused watching me fuck my boyfriend."

D: "Hmm…"

S: "What are you thinking?"

D: "Mostly about fucking you with an audience."

S: "Have a good night."

D: "You too."

DAY – 6

D: "Work was really rough last night. I'm exhausted."

S: "Why aren't you sleeping? Why are you up?"

D: "I wanted to talk with you. But when I think of you all I can think about is wild sex."

S: "I'd love to continue this conversation, but I've got to run. Want to talk later?"

D: "Sure. I'll call you this evening."

S: "Get some rest."

Day – 7

D: "Boy did I sleep yesterday. I must have really needed it."

S: "Good morning. Honestly, I don't know how you're able to function with your schedule."

D: "The answer is barely."

S: "How long do you think your company expects you to keep this up?"

D: "Wish I knew."

D: "I've got a doctor's appointment today. Just a checkup. How about you?"

S: "I have quite an exciting day planned for myself. Practice piano, work out, take the dog for a walk, then wait for a repair person. Ha!"

S: "I woke up at 3 am again thinking of you."

D: "Oh? What did you do?"

S: "What do you think? You might be interested to know that you have taken the place of the otherwise nameless, random man who would ordinarily be in my fantasy."

D: "Tell me about this fantasy."

S: "OK. But first, I want you to know that if you had been here with me I would have rubbed my bare breasts against your back as I reached over to gently stroke your cock to see if I could persuade you to touch me."

D: Mmmm..."

S: "And then I'm afraid that if that didn't work, I'd have to step up my game."

S: "Do you want more?"

D: "Yes, please."

S: "Well there would be so many things I can think of doing it's hard to decide. But I think I might rub my clit and get my fingers nice and wet. Then I'd waive them under your nose. Perhaps the scent of hot pussy might rouse you."

D: "It would definitely get me thinking."

S: "Then if that didn't work (but you know it surely would) my gentle stroking would become more aggressive and I might have to tease you with a few licks."

D: "Where?"

S: "On your magnificent cock, of course."

D: "God that would feel good."

S: "Yes it will. And I can't wait to have your cock in my mouth and drive you wild."

D: "Neither can I."

S: "You know, you're the only person I have ever sexted with. How am I doing?"

D: "Quite well. I'm stoking my cock every moment you're texting me."

S: "That really excites me. I'm going to have to do 5 extra miles on the bike just to function today. I wish you and your hard cock were here right now. I would love some intense action with you."

S: "But truth be known, I am a little nervous about having you for the first time."

S: "Do you want to know why?"

D: "Why is that?"

S: "Because your cock is so big and I'm so tight. What if we start and you can't penetrate me easily and I start saying "No, no," and that just excites you even more and you pin me down and force me to take all of you?"

D: "Is that exactly what you want?"

S: "I guess you'll have to wait and find out, but I'm starting to feel like we need a safe word. Because saying "no" while you continue doing what you like excites me greatly."

D: "Then we should have one."

S: "We'll have to come up with something. It needs to be easy to remember, but not a word we would generally use."

D: "How about 'ice cream?'"

S: "'Ice cream' it is. Just as long as it's not vanilla. I get bored easily."

D: "I'm quite sure it won't be."

S: "Me too. On a completely different subject, how much can you bench press?"

D: "Not very much. Last I checked it was 235."

S: "That's a lot! I'm just trying to figure out how athletic and gymnastic-like we can be with each other. You may be surprised. I'm in pretty good shape."

D: "I've been in better shape. This terrible schedule has taken a toll my body. But I'm working on getting back."

S: "What kind of music do you like?"

D: "I don't want to listen to music when I'm with you. I want to hear you breathe. I want to hear you moan and scream."

S: "OK. No music then."

S: "I'm on the Elliptical now. The time flies when I'm chatting with you."

D: "I'm sitting in my car waiting for the doctor's office to open and trying not to pull out my cock."

S: "Oh, how I'd love to do something for you in that car."

D: "I would love that."

S: "Then by all means we will. What kind of car do you drive?"

D: "Ford Escape."

S: "I like those. But for the kind of action I have in mind, we might need to use my car, because it's bigger inside I think. It's the Lexus LS."

D: "Mmmm, yes."

S: "We'll have to park some place that doesn't' have video surveillance. Otherwise, we might end up in trouble and on the 6 o'clock news with video clips to boot. LOL."

S: "Could you keep your eyes open to stand lookout while I suck your cock?"

D: "You said you like being watched."

S: "Only if there is no chance of arrest for public sex act."

D: "I would certainly try."

S: "Try? There can be no trying about it. Like NASA it would have to be "Failure is not an option.""

S: "Good luck at the doctor today."

D: "Hopefully it will be a quick visit."

S: "By the way, I have laughed so many times when the spell check on my phone substitutes a random word that would make no sense, especially in casual dialogue."

D: "Hahaha yeah that's happened more than a few times to me."

S: "I'm sure you'll ignore and forgive any typos on my part. But it does drive me crazy."

D: "Of course."

S: "I'm going to do weights, legs, now. Can we talk or text later?"

D: "Definitely. I'd love another pic."

S: "I'm sure you would. Bye for now."

Later that day the texting resumes.

D: "I just woke up hard as a diamond."

S: "Another waste of a perfectly good hard-on from my perspective. Can't wait to get my hands on you."

D: "Are you familiar with free use at all?"

S: "Only in copyright law. What is that?"

D: "Like the idea that if one of us is horny or just wants it, then the other obliges regardless of the situation."

D: "So for instance, you're folding clothes or something. I come over to you with an erection and I fuck you while you continue to fold clothes."

I bet he doesn't do much laundry.

S: "Baby that would just be called "Sara being Sara." I will never say no to you."

D: "Or we're out together and you just start rubbing my cock over my pants and get up and ride me until you cum."

D: "You might have to wear skirts all the time."

S: "I will tease you no matter where we are. I'll wear whatever you like."

D: "Maybe you could share me with one of your friends."

S: "I don't think I can share you."

D: "Doesn't mommy want to show off her son's massive cock?"

Oh no, here we go with the mommy stuff.

S: "You're so bad. I will have to devise special punishments for you."

D: "I just want mommy to share me with her friends."

S: "We'll see about that."

S: "I'm sure everyone will want you if they figure out what's between us."

D: "But I am your boy toy first and foremost."

S: "Aw shucks. Makes me want to give you a big kiss with my tongue thrusting into your mouth."

D: "Mmmm…"

S: "I hope you don't have the phone with you in the shower, son. Mommy wouldn't want you to get electrocuted."

D: "I'm standing outside while it warms up. And stroking myself.

S: "BTW, when is your birthday?"

D: "It just passed. It was February 15th."

S: "Happy belated birthday."

S: "OMG! You have the same birthday as my Mom. And I know all of the intricacies of your Aquarian nature. Did you know that our signs get along extremely well? Mine's Gemini."

D: "I did not."

S: "Did you know that Aquarian men are known to be open-minded, but shy and passive. And need passion intertwined with friendship?"

D: "No, but that might be true for me."

D: "I kind of want something special for our first time."

D: "My mind is going so many places. You in a chair, blind-folded, legs spread a part, waiting for me. Front door unlocked. I enter quietly and just watch you, torturing you with anticipation for a few minutes."

S: "I like that, go on…"

D: "We exchange no words. You hear me taking my cock out and stroking it. I approach you. You feel my proximity and start rubbing your clit more intensely in anticipation of what's coming."

D: "Your pussy is now aching for my cock. I position myself over you. You feel my breath on your neck, but I still haven't touched you. I lean in slightly and you feel the tip of my cock against the lips of your pussy."

D: "Still without touching you I begin to press and you start to feel it spreading your lips open. Your pussy is soaking wet and I know I could just slide the whole thing inside you."

S: "I'm going to cum again."

D: "I slide my cock up and down between your lips. Your fingers grip the arms of the chair in preparation for the thickness of my cock."

S: "Baby, you're driving me crazy."

D: "My cock now dripping with your wetness, in one smooth motion I thrust into you. I move to kiss you and our lips meet."

D: "You scream and moan into my mouth."

D: "I thrust over and over again, firm, hard, slow thrusts."

S: "How soon can you be here?"

D: "What do you mean?"

S: "I mean I want you as soon as possible in real life, touching me, doing all the things you're so skillfully teasing me with."

D: "If I could be there right now I would."

D: "I can't wait to hear you whisper a certain word when I enter you."

S: "What's the word you're longing to hear?"

D: "More a phrase I guess. I think you know it."

S: "I do and I will."

D: "That will make me cum instantly I think."

S: "I can't wait to have you cum, again and again."

D: "I have a fantasy of being your live-in fuck toy."

S: "Wow. Really?"

D: "Would you enjoy that?"

S: "I might just wear you out."

D: "Or maybe the other way around."

S: "And yes, I would."

D: "Your exercise bike might never get used."

S: "I can't wait to find out."

D: "I would be happy to buy some Cialis so I am always ready for you."

S: "Too funny. I don't think we'll need that. I'm fairly certain that I can keep you aroused.

D: "The spirit may be more than willing, but I would want to make sure that any second of the day I can please you, even immediately afterwards."

S: "I don't know what I will do with you. We may need to go somewhere for a few days and fuck till we can't move just so I can function again."

D: "Where would we go?"

S: "There are so many great options. But we'll need a sound-proof room."

S: "Have you ever tried the positions in the Kama Sutra?"

D: "Which ones are you thinking of?"

S: "Maybe we could try them all, one by one."

D: "I'd love that so much."

S: "I like the idea of sitting on your lap facing you while you penetrate me.

D: "I'm so glad you don't want to take it slow."

S: "What would be the point of that? It would be torture for me."

D: "And I can't stop thinking about you being into women."

S: "I'm glad that you like it and it excites you. I'm also glad that I can be open and honest and not have secrets."

D: "I do as well."

D: "I've cum twice since getting up this morning and I'm going to do it again."

S: "Where are you right now?"

D: "About to get into my car."

S: "You're such a bad boy."

D: "I'm going to stroke while I drive."

S: "Please don't have an accident."

D: "I won't mom. Sorry if I keep involving other women in my fantasies. I would make every moment, even if another woman was there, about what you want, what brings you pleasure."
S: "You're really something."
D: "I bet mommy has some friends she wants to fuck too."
S: "I probably need to jump off the phone now. I hope work goes well. I'll be thinking of you. Probably at 3 am again."

DAY - 8

After seven days of communicating with Declan, Sara notices that her jeans are falling off of her. When she gets on the scale, she's shocked. She's lost six pounds. Must have been those extra-long workouts she was doing trying to release all the energy she's been feeling.

Fuck diets. Women need to get young, hot lovers.

CHAPTER 3

Sex with an Intimate Stranger

• • •

THE FANTASY OF THE FIRST encounter. The night before Declan is supposed to come to Sara's house she can't sleep. Her restlessness isn't due to sexual fantasy this time. She's feeling very nervous about meeting him in the flesh. She's anxious about their first sexual encounter, wondering what it will be like. She's specifically worried whether his huge cock will fit inside her without ripping her apart. He seems like a wonderful person. She's not judging him from the messaging banter. It's their phone conversations. He's actually very respectful of her when they talk. And she's sure that when they meet if she decides that she doesn't want to have sex with him, he'll respect that. But what if she does want him, he starts fucking her, and she really can't take his massive size? How can you possibly expect a man to stop fucking you once you've already started? Is that reasonable? Is it realistic? Will he effectively rape her for real? *It's kind of like skiing. No matter how difficult or dangerous the mountain run might be, once your skis hit the slope you're committed for the long ride down. There's no turning back, like it or not.*

The next day, the doorbell rings at 7:00 a.m. *Well, this is it.* She opens the front door. There he is; her fantasy lover, in the flesh. Now he's not just a fantasy anymore. He's real.

S: "Hi there."
D: "Hi Sara."
S: "Come on in."

He crosses the threshold and looks her over from head to toe. She's wearing a very short skirt that's black with a delicate floral design. The skirt is flirty with layers of sheer fabric that move as she walks. She has on blush colored stilettos and a black skin tight tank top with the same black sweater she wore in the pic she sent him. She's wearing makeup. She looks pretty and sexy. He seems quite pleased with what he's seeing. She knows that he wants her to not wear panties. But she can't resist wearing them to feel the sensation of him pushing the soft, lace fabric aside to touch her and then ripping them off to have her.

"Would you like to have something to…"

Before she can finish her sentence, he grabs her and starts to kiss her passionately. She pulls her head away and laughs. It's nervous laughter. She's feeling overpowered by him already. He puts his hand on the back of her neck and pulls her so her face is towards his, as their mouths touch he parts her lips with his tongue. He's a great kisser. She sucks gently on his tongue. In his arms, she can feel his strength. He's very strong. Sex with him is going to be very athletic. She can sense and actually feel the passion and unbridled lust he has for her at this moment. *Everything is going to be alright. This is going to be amazing.*

When they stop kissing, she asks him if he'd like to sit in the living room for a little while.

"Let's get acquainted, huh?"

Sara is feeling intense and strange emotions. Declan is a stranger, but she feels that she knows him. *Why am I so nervous?* At a party last month, some of her friends were trying to list every man they'd ever slept with. Some of them had "guy at sports bar" on their list. *Why should I feel bad about this? I know him.*

Declan glances into the living room. It's a spacious room, with dark grey walls and a high ceiling. There's a large sofa, a beautiful tall wooden cabinet, a book case, and a piano.

"I want to hear you play piano. Play something for me."

"Really?" She laughs at the thought.

"All right, but just remember that I've only been playing for a few months. Don't expect it to be perfect."

"I won't."

She sits on the piano bench. He's stands behind her and places his hands on her shoulders. She wants him so badly she could jump right out of her skin. She has several piano music books, all different kinds of music she's been practicing. There's classical, popular, jazz, show tunes, and movie themes. "How about something from Phantom of the Opera? Do you know the story?"

"Not sure," he says with a sly smile.

She turns sideways so she can look in his eyes while she speaks to him. He walks a few steps away and takes a seat on the sofa. "Well, the music is extremely sensuous and erotic. I think it's meant to be played with a lot of passion and emotion and an understanding of when to when to pull back and when to really let go. So you have to know the story."

"The story takes place in late 1800's; at the Paris opera house Palais Garnier. Enter Erik, the Phantom of the Opera. He's a dark and mysterious man who wears a mask that conceals half of his face. OK, sadly, something is very wrong with his face. But I think the mask really represents his concealed true intentions. Anyway, he writes great operas that are performed and he generally terrorizes the Opera patrons."

"Along comes Christine Daaé. She's a young, beautiful virgin, who sings soprano and aspires to be an opera star. But her voice isn't great. Her father has died and she's now an orphan. Her father use to tell her Scandinavian fairy-tales, including one about the "Angel of Music.""

"The Phantom lives in a subterranean lair under the opera house. It's his hiding place, and really, it's his personal dungeon. He can't wait to get with Christine and bring her there. He becomes obsessed with Christine and starts calling for her while she sleeps. He gives her "singing lessons" in the middle of the night."

"Christine thinks that the phantom is the Angel of Music, giving her all kinds of tips and tricks so she can "perform better," which of course she does under his tutelage. Meanwhile, the Phantom is getting more and more sexual power over Christine. As Andrew Lloyd Webber puts it, "My power over you, grows stronger still.""

Enter Raoul, Christine's childhood friend and current sweetheart. When Erik finds out that Christine is in love with Raoul, he flies into a jealous rage and abducts her. He plans to keep her in his lair as his lover. The Phantom wants young Christine to stay with him in the world of darkness, which is code for seriously kinky sex, especially D&S. Soon, she's at the "point of no return" which means that if she doesn't get some soon, she'll die. Raoul is going to rescue Christine and take her out of the darkness and into the light. In other words, back to the world of boring, vanilla sex. Christine is kind to the Phantom, so he lets her and Raoul leave."

"It's a great story. She winds up going away with Raoul. Personally, I would have stayed with the Phantom. The sex would have been much better and you could star in his operas."

Sara's smiling and laughing again. Declan is amused by her. She begins to play *The Point of No Return*. It's a very appropriate song to mark the occasion for Declan and her. She plays quite well. Declan is a bit surprised that for a beginner she's able to play with such emotion. She plays through the piece without mistakes. She's been practicing.

When she finishes, Sara walks over to where Declan is sitting on the sofa. She sits on his lap facing him. He wraps his arms around her and begins to kiss her, deeply and passionately. He runs his fingers along her bare legs, from her ankles upwards, and underneath her skirt. When he reaches her panties, he looks at her with surprise.

D: "I half expected you wouldn't be wearing these."
S: "Well, a girl's got to do what she's got to do. I want to feel you push them aside."

He is responsive to her every desire. In that moment she feels the lace pushed aside as his fingers explore and finally touch her wetness. There are no words to adequately describe how excited she is for him at this very moment. It feels like every cell in her body is on fire.

Sara and Declan act out the sex scene they had fanaticized in their earlier text messages. They go up to Sara's bedroom. They undress quickly. On the bed, Declan lays on top of her. She feels the weight of his body and his hands touching her. She wraps her legs around him. He begins to penetrate her. It takes time. Even though she feels as though she can't take his massive size, she begs him to keep going. The sex is incredible.

The Reality of the First Encounter. It's President's Day. Sara wakes up before 5:00 a.m. unable to sleep thinking about Declan. Since she can't seem to successfully achieve climax by masturbating anymore, she decides to go work out. By 6:30 a.m. she's done 40 minutes on the exercise bike and 45 minutes on the Elliptical. Getting ready to do some weight work, she receives a text from Declan.

D: "How are you doing this morning?"
S: "I'm doing well. Finishing up working out. I've been waking up super early these days, even for me. I have a hard time lying around. I'd rather be doing something. Like trying to fascinate and excite you :)"

D: "If you give me a few I can call you and we can have some time to do exactly that…"
S: "I'll be waiting and anticipating our conversation."

Thinking that they're about to have phone sex, Sara continues her work-out while waiting for Declan's call.

D: "I really wish I could be naughty with you today."
D: "Maybe we could go and see a movie…"
S: "That would be great. Would we actually watch the movie? Or is it just a setting for an erotic adventure with my well-endowed lover?"
D: "More the latter? Would you actually like to do that today?"
S: "Well, I guess we'll need to sit in the back row and wear something that would enable me to slowly reach over and put my hand in the front of your pants."
D: "I don't have much outside of jeans."

OMG, what am I doing? Of course he only has jeans. He's so young.

S: "Well, the weather seems to be so ridiculously warm for February. Maybe when we go it will be warm enough for you to wear shorts. I might have to wear a very short skirt."
D: "What are your plans for the day? I want to see you."
S: "Sure. When?"
D: "I'm going to start heading to your place now."
S: "Now? I haven't even showered. I need a little time. And the house is a wreck."
D: "I don't care about the house. I'm coming to see you."
S: "OK. Can you give me an hour?"

D: "How are you going to greet me?"

S: "Well, I thought I'd come to the door and gauge your reaction when you first see me. I think we'll need to figure it out from there. If it doesn't work out, I'll make you breakfast. LOL. Can't wait to see you."

D: "My cock is already hard and in need of attention. My reaction will be accordingly."

S: "I see. I'll be in an extremely receptive mind set for you then."

D: "Mmmm…"

S: "Drive carefully, Baby. See you soon."

D: "You should read your story and get prepared."

S: "I don't know if we can get that crazy, but I'll improvise. I don't need a script. It's burned in my memory."

D: "What is our role play today? God I'm so excited. I know this is going to be incredible. I can't wait for you to grab me by the cock and make it belong to you."

D: "30 minutes away."

S: "OK, I may need a few more minutes."

D: "Can I park in the driveway?"

S: "Yes. I don't think the home owner will mind :)"

S: "How about if I open the front door when I'm ready? See you soon."

The house is actually very clean, but in disarray. Sara runs around like a mad woman straightening up as best she can. Then somehow she manages to take a shower, put on lotion and perfume, do her make-up and hair, and get dressed in less than 30 minutes; a true miracle. She goes down stairs and opens the front door. When Sara sees Declan walking from his car to the house she has second thoughts. *Oh my God. He looks so much younger than I was expecting. He looked older in the suit and tie. I think I was mistakenly picturing someone in his 40's.*

She opens the door wider. There he is; her fantasy lover in the flesh. Now he's not just a fantasy anymore. He's real.

S: "Hi there. Come on in."
D: "Hi Sara."

He crosses the threshold and looks her over from head to toe. She's wearing a very short skirt that's black with a delicate floral design. The skirt is flirty with layers of sheer fabric that move as she walks. She has on blush colored stilettos and a black skin tight tank top with the same black sweater she wore in the pic she sent him. She's wearing makeup. She looks pretty and sexy. He seems quite pleased with what he's seeing. She knows that he wants her to not wear panties. But she can't resist wearing them to feel the sensation of him pushing the soft, lace fabric aside to touch her and then ripping them off to have her. Before she can say anything, he grabs her and starts to kiss her passionately. He's a great kisser.

Sara is having work done in the house. The furniture in the living room is covered with drop cloths. She was expecting everything to be back in place by Friday when Declan arrived. Now they need to improvise.

S: "Would you like to do upstairs to my bedroom?"
D: "Absolutely."

The room is spacious and has a nice feeling to it. She has a king size bed. She's lit a large 3-wick candle that sits on the dresser. Its scent is light and fragrant. Declan takes Sara's hand, then pulls her in close to him, chest to chest. In his arms she can sense and actually feel the passion and unbridled lust he has for her at this moment.

Everything's going to be alright. This is going to be amazing.

He tears her clothes off as quickly as he can, when he sees her without her top and bra he gets a little wild.

S: "Am I what you were expecting?"
D: "Better than what I was expecting."

Sara feels relieved. She looks at him and can't believe they're about to have sex.

S: "If you didn't know me and you saw me on the street, would you think I was attractive?"
D: "Absolutely."
S: "Would you approach me?"
D: "No."
S: "Why not?"
D: "Because I would assume that you wouldn't be interested in me."

Sara smiles at him. *Interesting.*

Declan's handsome, but he's not really Sara's type. He has brown hair and green eyes, but he's a little shorter than she was expecting him to be. If they saw each other for the first time as strangers on the street, she doubts they would have even exchanged glances. But at this point, she's completely in lust with him and nothing else matters. She can't resist him. In her mind, he's become her perfect fantasy lover. They move toward the bed.

S: "Would you like to get into the bed, under the sheets or be on top of the blanket?"
D: "Let's start out on top."

He just wants to be able to see everything.

They get on the bed. She lies on her back. He's next to her, his body is touching hers. He studies her. He explores her body with his eyes, then his hands, then his mouth. He moves slowly and deliberately. He kisses her all over. He's in no rush. *Wow. He really is Indiana Jones, or at least his sexual version. He's on a great adventure; a quest to bring me as much pleasure as possible.* When he penetrates her for the first time, she can't believe the feeling. He fills her completely and then some.

S: "I think you might be too big for me."
D: "Don't worry, Baby. You'll get used to it."

She has a feeling he's right. They have amazing sex, a number of times. He deprives her of nothing. He fucks her in several different positions. When he takes her from behind, he gets so excited that he almost cums immediately. But he has control over himself. He stops for a second, and then slows down. He's not done with her yet. They change positions again. She has multiple orgasms. He cums all over her stomach. She loves it.

Sometimes, if you're really lucky, reality is better than fantasy. He's the best lover she's ever had, by far. He's coming back to see her on Friday as they had originally planned.

Later the same day they text.

S: "Baby, you're amazing. I'm not sure how it is that you've come into my life. But I'm really happy you have :)
D: "You are amazing. That was phenomenal."
S: "I'm glad the feeling is mutual. I thought I had calmed down. But thinking about what we just did has me aroused again. Friday seems like an eternity away. I want to be with you again."
D: "I love your pussy so much. I love how much you squirt."
S: "I'm blushing. It's a little embarrassing. I guess it means I can really let go when I'm with you. It turns me on that you like it."
D: "I do."

S: "I was half hoping that I would see you and come to my senses. But now I'm hopelessly consumed with thoughts of you. If someone had told me a month ago that life would take a turn like this I wouldn't have believed it."

D: "I'm having a bit of a difficult time concentrating on my work. I can't help but think about all the fun we will have. "

D: "Would you be open to including another woman ever?"

D: "I hope we do, it'd be the ultimate fantasy fulfillment for me."

S: "We need to talk about it. I'd certainly like to give you what you want. But, I truly want to end up in a relationship with a man. Women are like heroin for me. You like women too, I'm sure you understand. If I have sex with a woman again I don't know what might happen. And my future husband, if he exists and I can find him, might not be as understanding of my proclivity as you seem to be."

S: "And just out of curiosity, do you already have someone in particular in mind?"

D: "No, wish I did. And I get that. I don't want to ruin anything for you."

S: "I want more of you. Maybe rougher next time? Do you remember what you told me you wanted to do with pulling my hair, pushing me down, and taking me from behind? I want that and I want you."

D: "God I wish I was with you right now."

D: "I do remember."

CHAPTER 4

The Vignettes

• • •

PHONE CONVERSATION:

S: "Last night I stayed up all night writing. I'm writing a book about our relationship."

D: "That's hot. I like that. Can't wait to read it."

S: "I'll read it to you."

S: "So I thought I would create a number of role plays for us."

D: "And we can act them out."

S: "Yes, of course."

S: "I think I know some things you'd like."

D: "Like what?"

S: "Well one of them involves a student and her professor."

D: "Mmmm."

S: "She's on scholarship and does poorly on her midterm. She needs the professor to raise her grade. She's desperate."

D: "I see where this is going."

D: "You'll have to tell me more so I can come up with my lines."

S: "You don't need to worry about that. I can write the entire script. I'll read it to you. You can improvise if you want to. Lol."

D: "So every time we see each other we can do a different one?"

S: "If that would turn you on, yes."

<u>Preface</u>: The following fantasies were played out by the lovers as they explored some of their sexual desires. In the various roles, sometimes they are themselves, other times they're pretending to be other people; characters in the stories. Everything that happened was completely consensual. No one was seriously harmed in the execution of the fantasies. Neither of them required therapy afterwards. But their minds were turned a little inside out. It's role play time.

The Dancer

They're in her bedroom. Sara's chosen the perfect music for her performance; Sia's song "Move Your Body." The music is quick-paced, intoxicating, and makes you want to move. The lyrics are also on point. The song says that your body is poetry, asks - can't you see that I'm watching you and hot for you in every way, that I want to free you with my rhythm, and I can't get enough?

She has carefully chosen what to wear for this performance; a short, skin tight, black spandex skirt she can hike up over her hips with ease, black thigh-high stockings, stiletto heels, a black jacket, and a lacy black bra that unhooks in the front. For this performance she decides to forgo panties. She wants to drive Declan insane with desire.

She leads him to a chair she's placed about 10 feet away from where she'll dance. She wants him to be able to see her and take her in fully with his eyes. But she doesn't want him to be too far away either. Sara smiles at Declan and says "Before we begin, there are three rules. First, you can't touch me, until I say you can. Second, you can't touch yourself. Third, I can do anything I want. Do you agree to these rules?" Declan shakes his head in agreement. "Good." She smiles.

She turns on the music and turns her back to him. She slides her hands up a wall. There's a nice contrast between her red nails and the cream-colored paint. Although the music is very fast, she moves in a slower motion. She rotates her hips in an exaggerated way from side to side and then moves them in circles. Her hands wind their way down her body and along her legs, then up and across her buttocks. She steps one foot out so she can spread her legs a bit and arches her back so that her ass is somewhat tilted upward. *I wonder if Declan is already thinking about how he'll fuck me when I'm done.*

She turns toward him and can see that he's quite aroused, but pretends not to notice. She rocks her upper body and dips down to expose more of her cleavage. Still moving her body to the rhythm of the music, she reaches her hand down and stokes the length of one stocking-covered leg. She slides the skirt up just a little so Declan can see that she has nothing on underneath the skirt.

She takes her right index finger and puts it in her mouth sucking it in and out for a few moments. *Is he wondering what I'll do next or wishing that I was sucking his cock right now?* Then she runs her hands over her breasts and up to the back of her neck. Her right hand moves down over her abdomen and pulls up the front of her skirt. She runs her hand downward, slides a finger between her lips, and starts to rub her clit.

Declan is extremely engaged with the performance. She looks deeply into his eyes. *At this moment I have power over him.*

She walks over to him and straddles his right leg, being careful not to touch him just yet. After a few seconds, she sits down gently on his thigh and begins to grind on him rhythmically. She's driving him wild. He has the look in his eyes of a predatory animal waiting for just the right moment to pounce on its prey. Sara leans over and whispers in his ear, "Are you ready to fuck me now, Baby?"

"Yes, very much."

"Show me."

As he rises to stand he lifts Sara and throws her on the bed. *The power is all is his again.*

"Take off your clothes."

Sara rips off the jacket and bra in swift motions.

Declan grabs one of her legs and suddenly flips her over, pulling her lower body upward and towards him.

He smacks her ass hard.

"Owww!" she says in a voice that is almost a purr.

"You're such a little slut. You think you can tease me any way you want to?"

The sound of him unzipping his pants excites her.

"I think you need to remember who's actually in charge here."

He grabs her by the waist and thrusts his enormous cock inside her. She's so wet and excited that she takes the length of it. His cock hits her very deep inside. Her sounds become uncontrolled, guttural, and raw. She screams out in absolute ecstasy.

"You love my big cock inside you, don't you?"

"Yes…yes…I do. I love it. Please keep fucking me. Fuck me harder."

He fucks her very hard, over and over, until the two of them cum together. Then he leans over her and in a low growly voice whispers in her ear, "You are one sexy Bitch." They both laugh.

The Student and the Professor

"Hi Professor M" the girl says as she leans into the doorway of her Professor's office.

"I'm in your Tuesday/Thursday Theory class, I'm Katie."

"I'm pretty busy at the moment, Katie. Could you possibly make an appointment and stop by another time?"

"Well, I really need to talk to you today. It won't take but a minute. It's kind of important."

The professor waives his hand indicating that she should come inside the office. Katie enters and sits in the chair in front of the desk. The professor puts down the papers he's been reading.

"Well, you know, I love your class. It's so interesting. And I studied really hard for the mid-term. But I wound up with a C. I'm not really sure why I didn't do better. I really do know the material. And I never missed one of your classes."

"Sometimes that can happen. Maybe you can pull up your grade on the final exam."

"Well that's just the thing, Professor. You probably don't know this, but I'm at school on a full scholarship. If I don't keep a B average, I'll lose the scholarship. Without it, I can't be here. So my whole life kind of depends on it."

"I see."

"I was wondering if it might be possible for me to do something extra for you, like research or an extra paper, to bring my grade up."

"I have my research assistants for this year."

Katie gets up from the chair and stands closer to the Professor. She puts one hand down on the desk and leans toward him.

"Professor...I will do absolutely anything you say to raise my grade, anything. Just tell me what you want."

The Professor realizes that the day has just taken an unexpected turn. He becomes aroused.

"Well, that's an interesting problem and an interesting proposition. Why don't you go over to the door and lock it."

Katie walks across the room and locks the door.

"Check it."

She tries to turn the knob. The door is locked.

"Now come over here."

As she walks back toward the professor she wonders what's in store for her. He has a completely different look on his face. He looks stern. She suddenly feels frightened.

"You weren't planning on this today, were you?"

She shakes her head "No."

"Say "No, Professor.""

She looks downward and softly says, "No, Professor."

"Take off that top you're wearing."

She slides the t-shirt over her head and drops it on the floor. He gets up and walks over to her. In a quick motion, he unhooks her bra and tosses it near the shirt. He looks at her half-bare body, grabs both of her nipples, and squeezes them hard. She's frozen in place not sure what to do.

"You know Katie, you're a pretty girl. And I think a pretty girl like you...needs to be fucked in the face."

The professor walks to his chair, grabs a cushion he'd been leaning against, sits down, and tosses the cushion on the floor by his feet.

"I want you to get on your knees and suck my cock."

He looks at the cushion on the floor. She knows what's expected of her and she kneels before him.

"I want you to worship your Professor's cock."

He's already rock hard. She takes his cock in her hand and opens her mouth to draw it inside. But before she can do that, the Professor's hand is on the back of her head forcing her to take his cock faster and deeper into her mouth than she would have on her own. He's controlling her. He groans with pleasure as she's forced to take him in long deep strides and suck him over and over. He cums in her mouth. She swallows hard.

Once he's finished, he dismisses her.

"You can leave now. Please close the door on your way out."

Katie dresses quickly. She walks over to the door, stops, and turns back toward him.

"Professor, how did I do?"

"Let's put it this way, your scholarship is safe."

"Thank you, Professor. See you in class."

She opens the door and walks away.

MOMMY'S HOME

Theresa is in the kitchen contemplating what she'll make for dinner that evening. She's wearing a fancy black and white apron with ruffles. The word "Mom" is stitched in white lettering across the apron bib. All she's wearing under the apron is a black lace bra and matching panties. She's wearing black thigh high stockings and high heels. When her son Justin comes home he's a bit stunned by what his Mother is wearing. She has a great body, which he can see quite well.

T: "Hi there, Baby. How was your day?"

J: "It was good."

T: "Baby, why don't you have a snack, then I want you to do something for me. I'm going to go upstairs in a few minutes. When I do, wait 10 minutes, then you come upstairs too. When you find the room I'm in don't come into the room. Just stand by the door. I want to talk to you, OK?"

J: "Sure."

T: "Oh and Honey, please take out the trash after you have your snack. And make sure you wash your hands when you come back inside."

Theresa heads up stairs. After waiting 10 minutes, Justin follows. He finds that his Mother is running the shower. The bathroom door is partly open. He stands outside the room as he was instructed. He peeks in and sees that his Mother is naked under the running water. The water is streaming over her body. Steam from the heat of the water blurs her image just a little. She's rubbing soapy lather all over her body.

T: "I know you're there, Baby... And I know that this isn't the first time you've peeked in on me in the shower. You really like what you see, don't you?"

J: "Yes."

T: "I can't decide whether I should punish you …or have you join me in this shower. Maybe I should turn you over my knee and give you a sound spanking. You're never too old to be spanked, you know. Is your cock nice and hard for me, Baby?"

J: "Yes, it is."

T: "Well then, I think you should come in here with me. I've been waiting for you."

Justin takes off his T-shirt and jeans, opens the shower door, and gets inside. He can't believe that this is actually happening. He's fantasized about it so many times. He grabs her and touches her body. Her breasts feel so good in his hands. He works his fingers down to her pussy and plunges two fingers deep inside. She moans. He turns her around. Her hands are on the shower wall. As he starts to fuck her hard from behind, she turns her head towards him and says, "Is this what you've been wanting, Baby?" He nods. "Good. And you feel so good. Go ahead Baby, cum for Mommy."

As she says the words, he becomes instantly crazed and fucks her as hard as he can. Then he suddenly pulls out and explodes shooting his load all over her. Good thing they've in the shower. They rinse off. She opens the door, grabs a towel, and steps out onto the shower mat.

T: "Why don't you get cleaned up and dressed. I'll see you down stairs for dinner in a little while."

J: "Yes, Ma'am."

T: "And Justin, let's keep this our little secret. OK?"

J: "OK, Mom."

The Mirror and the Chair

In her bedroom, there is a very large mirror over the dresser. She's standing in front of the mirror looking at herself. Her hair is swept up in a twisted knot. Some of the loose curls frame her face. She's wearing a long, red silk robe. The silk is very soft and feels sensual against her skin. She has nothing on under the robe. She's wearing black stiletto heels.

Her lover is lying on the bed against a row of pillows. He's reading CNN on his tablet. He's barefoot wearing khakis and a T-shirt.

"Baby, come over here. Would you please?"

He looks at her and puts down the tablet. He gets up and walks across the room to join her.

"Come stand behind me, close."

He comes up behind her, wraps his arms around her, and looks at the reflection of the two of them in the mirror.

"I want you to open my robe, slowly. Then I want you to touch my body. I want to watch you touching me."

A devilish smile spreads across his face as he starts to untie the belt. He pushes the soft fabric to the sides of her body so that her breasts are fully exposed. She leans back against him and can feel his hard cock pushing against her ass.

"You look so fucking hot, Baby."

He touches her face. She grabs his right hand and kisses it. She turns his hand over and kisses and playfully bites his palm. She runs her tongue around his wrist and kisses the places her tongue has been. Then she takes his first two fingers, licks them, and then sucks them in and out of her mouth. She moves his hand down to her abdomen. He kisses the back of her neck. It's a very erogenous area. The more he kisses her there, the more aroused she becomes.

"Touch me. Please Baby, touch me."

He moves his hands to her breasts, first cupping them, and then teasing her nipples pinching and pulling on them. He slides one hand down her abdomen, parting her lips to touch her clit. He begins to rub it back and forth, then in firm circles. She is immediately wet and her clit is hard.

"I love watching you move your hands all over me."

She slides her hands forward on the top of the dresser and leans toward the mirror suggesting to him that perhaps he should fuck her from behind at that very moment. But she actually has other plans. He presses his cock against her ass, hard. As he starts to pull her robe off, she takes his hand and leads him to a chair she's placed in the room.

"Sit down, Baby."

He doesn't say a word as he takes the seat. She unbuckles his belt, unzips his pants, and helps him slide his pants and briefs down so he can kick them off. He pulls his T-shirt over his head and tosses it to the floor. She drops to her knees directly in front of him. She looks into his eyes as she firmly grasps the shaft of his cock in her hand.

"I love sucking your cock."

"I love it too." He laughs. "You're amazing."

She keeps looking into his eyes as she takes the head of his cock into her mouth, playfully licking and kissing. Her lips are very soft. As she wraps them around his cock he moans. Her tongue licks downward as she continues to suck. Her hand moves in a circular motion jerking him hard as her mouth almost meets her hand on his cock. He leans further back in the chair. When he is completely aroused, she takes him deeper into her mouth. He's moaning. He's in man heaven.

"That feels incredible. Don't stop…don't stop. Mmmmm."

He doesn't need to tell her what to do. She has no intention of stopping, just yet. She continues the firm, circular jerking motion while her tongue dances up and down, as she sucks him hard. After a few minutes she can tell that he's about to cum. She stands up, drops the robe on the floor, and straddles his lap. He reaches down to touch her. She's dripping wet. First one, then another, he slides two fingers inside her. As she moans, he fucks her repeatedly, in and out with his fingers. Then in a sudden motion he pulls his fingers out and pushes his rock hard cock inside her. She rocks her lower body back and forth. She squeezes his cock as hard as she can as she moves.

"I love it when I can feel you squeeze my cock with your pussy."

"I want you to cum in me. Come on, cum for me, Baby."

She puts her thumb on his lips and pushes it into his mouth. He sucks on it as they fuck. Suddenly, he grabs her hips and starts to fuck her harder, pushing her down onto his cock.

"You feel so good, Baby. You're fucking amazing."

"I want you to cum so hard that I can feel your cock pulsing inside me."

They both explode. He fills her with his hot juice. And she drenches him with hers.

THE PLUMBER

Mike the plumber had been to her house before. It was just a minor issue with a sink. He was so polite and professional. He definitely made a positive impression on Andi. She watched him as he worked. He's rugged and super strong. He spent a lot of time that day talking with her. More time, she imagined, than he likely spent with his other clients.

A month later, a fairly serious plumbing issue happens with an outside pipe. It's evening. All Andi can do is to shut off the water main. She calls the plumbing company right away. Because it's a Saturday evening, she's told that the earliest anyone can be at the house is the next afternoon.

On Sunday morning at 7:00 a.m., the phone rings.

A: "Hello."
D: "Hello Andi. This is Mike, the plumber."
A: "You recognized my voice. Hi Mike, How are you?"
D: "I'm fine. I see that you're having a plumbing issue."
A: "Yes. There's a leak in an outside pipe."
D: "Well, they have you on the list for later today. But the notes say that you have no water."
A: "I had to shut the water main off to stop the leak."
D: "I'm going to move you up and see you first."
A: "Thank you Mike. That's really nice of you."
D: "See you in about 45 minutes."
A: "Thanks. Bye."

As she hangs up the phone, she thinks about how cute Mike is. She wonders whether he'll be as friendly to her today as he was the last time she saw him. She decides to exercise while waiting for him to arrive. She's wearing skin tight yoga shorts and a form fitting V-neck T-shirt.

When Mike rings the doorbell, Andi grabs a polar fleece jacket and quickly puts it on. She doesn't zip the jacket. He comes inside the house. He's wearing his navy blue plumber's uniform. His name is embroidered on a patch above the left pocket of his shirt.

A: "Hi Mike, come on in."
D: "Good morning. Let's take a look at that pipe."

Andi walks outside with Mike and into the back yard. She points, showing him where the leak is located.

D: "OK. Now let's go inside and see the shutoffs."

Ordinarily, at this point, Andi would have left the plumber to do whatever work is needed. But she was happy to spend time being around Mike. They walk back into the house to the basement where the water main is located. Mike takes a look at the pipes.

D: "You should have been able to shut off the outside water without turning all the water off. Come over here. I want to show you."

Andi walks over to where Mike is standing. There really isn't enough room for two people in the small space. She's standing very close to him. She notices him checking out her cleavage. She senses that he's very attracted to her. He shines a small, but powerful pen light on the shutoff lever.

D: "See, this is the lever you should have shut off. Whoever put these pipes in should have marked them for you."
A: "I see."
D: "Don't worry. I'll tag everything before I leave today."
A: "Thank you."

Mike takes a hard look at Andi's body.

D: "You look really amazing."
A: "Thanks. I've been working out a lot."
D: "Well it really shows. You looked great before. But now, wow."
A: "Thank you."
D: "You know that if I had known yesterday that you were without water, I would have come over here at midnight to take care of this problem."

A: "Really. How would your wife feel about you leaving home so late?"

D: "I'm not married," he says with a smile.

A: "Well, at the risk of losing the best plumber I've ever had, I need to tell you that if you had come over here at midnight, I would've had other things for you to do than work on that pipe."

D: "Is that a fact?"

A: "Yes, it is."

In one swift motion, he grabs her and pulls her to him. It's a surprise to Andi and she gasps. They move out of the confined space.

D: "You know I wanted you the first time I was over here."

A: "Really?"

D: "Absolutely."

A: "Why didn't you say anything?"

D: "Well, it's a tough situation. If I hit on you and you're not into it, you could turn around and sue the plumbing company for harassment. I have to be very careful. But I was hoping you'd make a move."

Andi grabs him and kisses him hard. He plunges his tongue into her mouth. She runs her hands over his biceps. He's very muscular. All that lifting on the job has paid off. Mike lifts Andi up and she wraps her legs around him. With one hand he pulls the front of her T-shirt downward, slides his hand inside her bra, and touches her nipple. Andi is very aroused.

"We need to take off those shorts you're wearing."

He puts Andi down and she takes off all of her clothes. Mike looks at her and kisses her neck while fondling her breasts. She reaches down and begins to stroke his firm cock through his work pants. He unbuckles his belt, unzips his pants, and slides them down. He lifts Andi again and presses her back against a wall. When he reaches down to touch her, he discovers that she's very wet. He rams his cock inside her hard, again and again. She moans and screams as he continues to pound into her. The encounter is very exciting to both of them. They cum together. Afterwards, Andi fumbles with her clothes trying to get dressed quickly.

"I guess I'll get back to work now. I'll have that leak fixed in no time."

"Thank you, Mike. You know, you really are the best plumber ever."

Ravish me

She's a woman who doesn't care much about being cuddled. She just wants to be taken by him, forcefully. She knows exactly what to say to instigate the action she craves.

"You think you can have me whenever you want. But you can't."

He sees the smirk on her face.

"Is that so?"

He pushes her down on the bed and gets on top of her. She feels the weight of his body pressing into her and she becomes aroused. He grabs hold of both her wrists with one of his hands and pushes them over her head, holding them there. That small assertive motion drives her further into a fantasy of surrender and submission. He engulfs her. She feels his size and the strength from his masculine energy. Hers pale in comparison. He whispers to her, "Don't resist me. You won't be able to. I'll take exactly what I want from you." She moans. "You're my little slut, only mine. I'll do whatever I want with you."

He has to have her. His desire is carnal. Her mind dances in several directions. She wonders what he'll do to her next. His passion for her has made her feel more adventurous. He touches her body then kisses her, starting at her neck and working his way down to her breasts. He kisses then gently bites her nipples. He's forceful and aggressive. His attention is completely focused on her body. The line between pleasure and pain has become blurred for her. She wants to feel his strength. She wants to feel like she's in another place, a different dimension. In that place she can let go, because he's completely in charge. She has no choice. She's free from any thoughts or distraction that might hold her back from feeling compete ecstasy.

He starts to open her legs with his and she resists pushing her legs together.

"I told you not to fight me. You'll never win."

He quickly forces her legs open wide with his. He presses against her and she can feel how hard he is. Her body can't resist him. He begins to penetrate her and she surrenders to him. It seems like the more she gives in to him, the more he wants to take. He stares into her eyes. They breathe in unison. "Say, "Do whatever you want to me." I want to hear you say it. Go on, say it. "Do whatever you want to me."" She repeats the statement in a whisper. "Do whatever you want to me."

He reaches his hands underneath her and grabs her ass as he continues to thrust his cock into her, fucking her hard. Then he raises his body, takes hold of her legs and places them over his shoulders. He begins to pound in and out of her, harder and harder. He's looking into her eyes. His eyes are animalistic. He looks driven by some unknown force. She's so overwhelmed by him it's hard for her to continue meeting his gaze and she closes her eyes.

"Look at me. I want you to keep your eyes open and look at me while I'm fucking you."

He is completely in charge. She obeys him, opens her eyes, and forces herself to meet his gaze. She feels an intense rush of emotion. She knows that at this moment she is his sole focus. That thought takes her away from the here and now. She's in the dimension of pounding heart beats, quick breaths, and wetness between her legs. All the while, he's pounding into her rhythmically, over and over again. In complete restraint, she is totally free. He comes inside her as she explodes for him.

CONCLUSION

•••

YOU MIGHT BE WONDERING WHAT happened to the relationship with Declan. After a while, he just disappeared. When one day he didn't show up to meet me, I sent him a text.

> S: "I can't remember the last time I was stood up. I'm going to assume that you've been sent away on a secret mission, swept away by a flood or suddenly remembered that you have a wife and 3 children. If you still want to see me, please let me know. If not, I'd rather not have my mind completely wrapped around you. If you've decided this situation isn't right for you, just let me know. Maybe I can go out with some other man and see if I can break the spell you currently have over me."

I never heard back from him. At first, I thought that maybe something had happened to him and I was worried. But I didn't make any effort to find him. I'm fairly certain I could have found him if I'd tried. After all, I know where he works. Whatever happened, Declan decided to stop seeing me. And I accept that. Maybe he found someone else. Maybe whoever it is, she's willing to have group sex. Maybe living his darker fantasy was too much for him. Or maybe he knew I couldn't live it for him on a day-to-day basis. I don't know. I don't make up stories in my head about reality. I save that strictly for fantasy. Sometimes in life you just don't get answers to your questions.

The thing you don't know is that in between all of the sex talk, we had other conversations. We discussed politics, religion, music, technology, books we read, and our lives. Declan is extremely intelligent. And I really enjoyed talking with him. Of all things, it was actually his intelligence that attracted me to him the most. I think of him as having been my friend. I really do care for him. I wish that he had said "Good bye." Although I knew from the beginning that a relationship with him would never last, the end of the relationship made me feel sad.

Meeting "Declan" was a complete surprise. Becoming involved with him was a life changing experience. Despite how hot the story is, it wasn't the sex that was life altering, but the way the relationship caused me to change my perceptions. I'm healthier, happier, and look better now than I did before I met him. I'm glad he came into my life. He's a great person. He'll always have a special place in my heart. In the end, that's all that really matters to me.

AUTHOR'S POST SCRIPT

• • •

I HOPE THAT YOU'VE ENJOYED reading *Love Map* as much as I enjoyed writing it. You may be wondering whatever possessed me to write this book. I guess I just had an unexpected and extraordinary experience that was too good to keep to myself. The spirit moved me and I wrote this book in little more than 30 days. This isn't the first book I've written. But it's the first one in this genre. I also hope you won't judge me too harshly for the content here. It's honest. It's what's happening today in our world.

Why did I have this experience? Who can really say? I'm basically just like everyone else. I'm a complex person with a complicated life. I work a demanding job, take care of other people and pets, pay my bills and taxes, and do all the things generally expected by society. I've spent most of my life playing inside the lines, always following the rules. Just like you, I have feelings and emotions. For a long time, I focused so much energy on my work that there was little time left over for anything or anyone else. Although work brings me satisfaction and I feel like I'm helping others, I've often felt like something is missing and wondered if there isn't more to life.

A few months before I decided to try Internet dating, I was truly inspired by the physical metamorphosis Wendy Williams had made. I looked at her and thought that if she could slim down and look great, so could I. So I kicked my workouts into high gear, doubling the cardio.

And I changed my diet. I cut out sugar and almost all bread and dairy. Within a very short time, I had dropped my weight and felt fantastic. That boost gave me the confidence I needed to start dating again. Thank you, Wendy!

When *50 Shades of Grey* came along, I became deeply troubled that women would feel compelled to submit to abuse in order to sexually please a partner. It's true that sometimes being a little naughty and getting spanked can be a huge turn on. But while the fantasy of complete sexual surrender suggests otherwise, there's nothing erotic about being beaten or tortured. And when you allow another person to use restraints on you, you place your life in their hands.

I think that women who read my book just might claim or recover their power. I hope they'll realize that being strong is sexy and that they can take some control over their sexual activities. The themes in this book are some of the many secret desires that men and women fantasize about. The book just verbalizes them. The role play fantasies are on the shorter side and get into the action of sex almost immediately. This is completely intentional on my part. While women may enjoy romance novel style writing with lots of details leading up to the sex acts, most men do not. And you can't act out all of the lead in material. This book is intended to appeal to men and women. So, I made a conscious decision to keep the romance novel aspects to a minimum. Note that Declan is not described in detail in the fantasies or anywhere else in the book to protect his identity and privacy.

If you're intrigued by role play you might want to give it a try. Just remember that as in all things in life, you get out of it what you put into it. So before you get started, discuss what you want to do with your lover. Make sure both of you find the idea enticing. Next, consider what you need to make the scene seem real; props, certain clothing, lighting, music, etc. Then read the scenario together. Practice it individually. You don't have to memorize it, but make sure you know the direction of the story so you can ad lib something close. You can also practice it mentally, by closing your eyes and imagining how it will go. Last, if you really want to make this a great experience, don't leave it as an afterthought at the end of the day when both of you are too tired to really enjoy it. Make time for yourselves. And have fun. I want to drop a footnote here: Please practice safe sex, the stories in this book notwithstanding. The book is, after all, at least part fantasy.

There are two things I've learned in life that I know are true. First, life is unpredictable. Second, everything, good and bad, is temporary. So I hope that if life's got you down, that this book made you laugh a little and maybe have some fun. Why not fantasize? As long as you're with a consenting adult and you're not hurting anyone else, what's the harm? Getting out of your comfort zone and playing adult games may feel good to you. So why not use this book as your mental sex toy? If it appeals to you and your spouse, partner or lover, try the role play out for size. Fantasy can change your sex life forever.

It would be great if more people used their imaginations to take an occasional mental vacation from the stress of reality. Maybe they could release some of the negative emotions so many people seem to carry around. If they did, perhaps fewer people would self-medicate with drugs and alcohol or take anti-depressants so they won't feel their emotions. Sorry, there's that pesky Gemini in me wanting to share information again. At least I come by it honestly.

Life is so wonderful and full of surprises. I've come to expect the unexpected. And you never know what could happen next. This book could become wildly popular. Then someone could decide to turn the book into a movie. And Wendy Williams could invite me to be on her TV show to talk about the story behind the book. She'll invite Josh Groban to be the musical guest. He'll perform the song *Awake*, because Wendy's read the book and she's told Josh that I have crush on him and that the song is one of my favorites.

You know, I'm not some crazy obsessed fan. I've only been to one of Josh's concerts. It was the one at Wolf Trap National Park in Vienna, Virginia, a few years ago. I enjoyed it very much. His voice is so beautiful and the level of emotion he sings with is so intense, it made me cry. The concert aside, I have watched several of his interviews. I think he's handsome, very intelligent, extremely talented and creative, and funny. And he's silly sometimes, like I can be. Some of the things he's said in his interviews resonate with me. He mentioned how opportunity can be easily lost and how losing nervousness can impact performance. These are life lessons that most people might not learn until their 40's, if they learn them at all. And for goodness sake, the man spent time with Nelson Mandela. He's done so much in his life already that his chronological age is far behind his life experiential age. Maybe he finds women his own age boring. He might enjoy the company of an older woman. You never really know what could be percolating below the surface of a person.

So if all of that is true, maybe later the evening of the Wendy show, Josh and I will have dinner together and a couple glasses of wine. We'll get to talking and laughing. And we'll find out a little bit about each other. Who knows where that might lead? Now that's a fantasy. And it's mine. In the meantime, I'm going to learn to play one of Josh's songbooks on the piano. I love the music, but it's hard for me to play, because I've only been playing for a few months. But that doesn't matter. I'll master it. I'm highly motivated. And I like to practice…a lot.

I wish you well.

I welcome your comments and questions. Please feel free to contact me at: Alice@Lovemapnow.com

SOME OF THE PHOTOS ALICE
SENT TO DECLAN

• • •

ALICE ELLISON IS THE NOM de plume of the author, a successful trial attorney based in Washington, DC. *Love Map*, her novel, is based on a true story.